FLYING DUO

ZOE MAY

CONTENTS

1 CHAPTER ONE

Dear Miss Watson,

We are writing to inform you that you are no longer permitted entry to the Hridaya Ashram.

In light of the recent court case between yourself and Guru Hridaya, we have come to the conclusion that your presence is detrimental to the calm and peaceful atmosphere that we aim to cultivate here. For this reason, you will not be allowed to attend workshops, eat at the ashram's restaurants, cafes or canteen or use any of the ashram's facilities.

You are now banned from setting foot on the ashram's premises entirely and any violation of this ban will result in your immediate removal from the ashram by force.

I hope you understand that we feel this is

the most appropriate course of action.

Regards,

Rahul Manshif

Ashram Manager

I stare at the letter, eyes wide. *Banned?* Who gets banned from an ashram?!

I look up from the letter at the view of the sea through the window above my desk. I usually find the sight of the Indian Ocean shimmering under the sun soothing, but instead of admiring the rolling waves, I instead catch sight of my own reflection in the glass. I look as bewildered as I feel.

Okay, so I might have worked with a local law firm to sue the guru of the ashram over tax evasion, resulting in him having to pay back fifty million rupees to the Indian government, but I mean, banned?! That's just rude. It's not exactly like I hang out there anyway. I get that I'm not entirely welcome, and I've been far too busy lately to take part in any yoga classes. But still, the tone of the letter – its passive aggressive forcefulness makes me feel a bit strange. A bit rejected. I may not approve of the ashram and its practices, but I found myself at a time when I was really lost in that ashram.

I didn't come to the ashram to find myself, like most people do. In fact, I came to try win my boyfriend back. My ex, Paul, had grown tired of our life together back in London and so he decided to break up with me and jump on a plane to India to take some time out. Devastated from having been dumped, I decided to try to prove to him that I could be free-spirited and adventurous too and came all the way over here in an effort to patch things up between us. Except things didn't exactly go according to plan. Firstly, Paul was outraged that I'd dared to follow him to India. He thought it was weird and stalkerish, which is kind of fair. At the time, I was so heartbroken that it felt like the right thing to do. And secondly, he moved on from me quicker than you can say 'enlightenment'. When I got here, he was already dating an American hippy called Blossom. Feeling like a complete fool, I wanted to jump on the first plane home, except I couldn't change my flight and I ended up stuck in India for two weeks. I sulked around the ashram for a few days, but after a while, I started to quite enjoy it. I warmed to this place. I started to enjoy the birdsong in the mornings and the peaceful, relaxing way of life. I met some interesting people who opened my eyes to new things like meditation and mindfulness, and before I knew it, I was coming to terms with the end of my relationship and realising that it was actually me who had needed to find herself.

I met Seb too. He was staying at my guesthouse and took me under his wing, being a true friend to me during that confusing time, but then we started to fall for each other, even though in many ways we're total opposites, with me being an extremely driven corporate lawyer from London and him a curious and slightly directionless spiritual seeker from Montreal. But despite our differences, we fell in love. We got to know each other while walking along the ashram's winding terracotta paths and hanging out in each other's treehouse rooms. I couldn't believe it when I rocked up at the guesthouse and realised the room I'd booked was literally up a tree – a small treehouse covered in bamboo leaves, and yet I grew to love staying there. I have great memories of the place and now, I'm banned.

I know the letter is just a snub, a mean and petty way to get back at me for winning the court case. So much for enlightenment. I toss the letter onto the coffee table behind me with a sigh and go outside to sit on the balcony of the flat I now share with Seb. When we first got together, we were both staying in the ashram, but then I started working on my lawsuit against the ashram founder, Guru Hridaya, and we knew we had to move. We got a cute ramshackle flat in the city of Pondicherry a few miles away from the ashram site. The town used to be a French colonial settlement and the architecture reflects that legacy, with quirky mustard-coloured houses and tall white weather-beaten townhouses with blue shuttered windows facing the sea. Seb and I got a flat right by the seafront with a balcony overlooking the beach. Whenever I'm stressed, I go out and sit on the balcony and watch the waves come and go. The steady gentle ebb and flow is always calming.

I hear the pad of Seb's footsteps behind me and turn around. He's been meditating in the next room and he seems a little dazed as he often is when he's been meditating for a while. It's almost like waking up from sleep for him.

'What's up?' Seb asks. 'You look down.'

'Oh.' I force a smile, but it probably looks as laboured as it feels.

I give up. Seb sits down in one of the wicker chairs as I lean against the balcony rails.

'I just got a letter from the ashram informing me that I'm permanently banned and if I go back I'll get "removed by force",' I explain.

'Removed by Force?' Seb echoes, his mouth twisting into a smile. He looks like he's trying not to laugh.

'It's not funny!' I insist, although Seb starts laughing regardless.

I roll my eyes, although I reluctantly find myself smiling too, beginning to see the funny side. I've been banned from an ashram. That is quite an achievement.

'They said I was "detrimental to the peace and ambience",' I tell Seb.

He snorts with laughter.

'Sorry!' he says, in between giggles.

I can't help laughing. I sink down into the wicker chair next to him.

'It is kind of funny, I suppose,' I say. 'But I do feel a bit like an outcast now.'

Seb stops laughing and turns to me, a sympathetic look in his eyes. 'You did know this was going to happen though, didn't you?' he asks.

'Well, I didn't think I'd be outright *banned*. I thought myself and Guru Hridaya had a tacit understanding that we'd stay out of each other's way,' I tell him. 'Being banned just feels weird.'

Seb shrugs. 'Well, I guess they just wanted to make it official. They're annoyed they lost the lawsuit and I suppose this is their way of getting back at you.'

'Yeah, I guess,' I sigh.

Seb reaches over and squeezes my knee.

'Don't let Guru Hridaya get to you! You're better than him,' he assures me, with a sweet smile.

He's right. Guru Hridaya is incredibly corrupt. He claims to be an enlightened, modern-day incarnation of Shiva and yet when he's not at the ashram, he's driving a Ferrari, living in a mansion and leading a life of Hollywood-style excess. He's spent years collecting donations from his followers and charging tourists extortionate amounts for self-discovery courses and yet he hadn't paid a penny of tax, meaning that despite the ashram bringing thousands of visitors to the area every month, the streets were run down, pitted with potholes and spattered with litter. He thought he could get away with it, assuming that no one would challenge him in court, but my law firm specialises in tax evasion and fraud cases and we took on the case.

'I know I'm better than Guru Hridaya, but we just had so many happy memories at the ashram that it feels a bit weird to be shut out,' I comment.

Seb smiles sympathetically.

I know the letter shouldn't really affect me and that it is a bit petty, but I do feel a bit put out. Perhaps it's having how unwelcome I am spelt out in black and white that's making it feel more cutting and real. Life around here revolves around the ashram. It's the beating heart of the community and now I'm officially banned. It makes me feel like maybe I should move on. Maybe the time has come to leave India. My firm insisted I take some time off after the gruelling case. They suggested that if I'd like to, perhaps I could take on some more cases over here, get a work visa, but I'm beginning to feel that it might be time to leave. But where do I go from here? What's next not only for me, but for me and Seb?

I've been so busy with the legal case lately that I haven't given that much thought to our future. We've been so happy together so far. Ever since we met, we've been inseparable. Back when we were at the ashram, we were staying in the same guesthouse, spending pretty much every day and night together, and then we moved to this little flat and we've been each other's world here too. I thought it might be make or break moving in together, away from the community at the ashram and all of its distractions, but it's been amazing. Instead of boring each other or getting on each other's nerves, Seb and I have just grown closer. I've grown to love our daily routine of waking up, lying in each other's arms, the sun streaming in through the windows, before eating breakfast on the balcony. I've done most of my work on the case in the flat, communicating with a law firm in Mumbai and my company back home online. Sometimes I've even worked on the balcony, the sun warming my arms as I type, the sound of the waves lapping away at the shore in the background. Seb is from Montreal and is fluent in French and English and so he's been doing some freelance translation work. He even went up to Mumbai recently for a meeting with a tech company looking to expand their business to France and he's had loads of work from them since. He doesn't particularly love sitting in front of his computer, but we make up for it in the evenings, when we go for walks along the beach or if it's particularly hot, a swim. We don't have a TV and when the sun's gone down, sometimes I'll join Seb in meditation or we'll sit and read together, the flat lit by tea lights and smelling of incense.

It's been heavenly and a complete contrast to my life back in London – the crowded Tube journeys, the dull suits and corporate offices, the evenings spent in front of the TV, scrolling on Facebook.

It's not just the lifestyle that I've fallen in love with, but Seb. I've fallen for him in a big way. He knows I love him. We told each other the first day we moved into this flat. We were sitting together on the balcony, curled up under a blanket, watching the sun set and the words just tumbled out of us. We were both on exactly the same page: completely and utterly in love. But even though I know Seb adores me as much as I adore him, we haven't really discussed the future. Seb is all about living in the moment, and while that's great and everything, it's also, kind of anxiety-inducing at times too. The deeper in love I've fallen with him, the more I've begun to wonder what our long-term plans are, and the more I've felt I haven't been able to ask without ruining the magic. I love what we have, and I haven't wanted to burst our bubble by having that conversation. We've been together for around six months now. Most couples don't have to discuss their future in such serious terms after just six months, but Seb and I will have to.

Seb's from Quebec and I'm from southeast London. Our visas will eventually run out and even though life over here is amazing, I do sometimes feel like a bit of a runaway. I miss my friends back home, my family, my lovely house. But if I go back to London, where does that leave me and Seb? Will we go our separate ways, consigning our relationship to an incredible holiday romance? Are we going to try to have a long-distance thing? Or are we going to decide to settle down together either in London or Quebec, which would be a serious commitment to make for a relatively new relationship. I've contemplated moving to Quebec and while I would if I had to, to be with Seb, I'd rather we settled in London. I'm a partner at my law firm in the City and it's a job I've worked extremely hard for. My career has always been important to me, whereas Seb is a bit lost. He's really intelligent, but he hasn't quite settled on a career path yet. It would make a lot more sense for us to move to London, where I have a good job and a house. But the conversation is so big and fraught that I keep avoiding it. What if we realise that despite loving each other, we have to go our separate ways? That would be so heart-breaking.

'Don't feel like a pariah,' Seb says, no doubt noting the troubled expression on my face. He clearly thinks I'm still upset about the letter. 'You're a local hero,' he adds.

I laugh.

I'm not exactly a local hero, but there are quite a few people in the community that appreciate the work that I put in to get Guru Hridaya to start paying tax. The story's been in the local papers with my picture a few times and sometimes as I'm walking around town, one or two of the locals will give me a respectful nod or I'll receive little tokens of thanks like a free loaf of bread in the bakery or a cup of chai in shops. It's nice, but then on the flipside, there are also ashram dwellers and devotees of Guru Hridaya who don't particularly approve of me, believing I've tarnished the name of their beloved guru. They all wear white robes – the clothing of choice of the guru's devotees – and often when I pass them, they'll shoot me dirty looks, which can be quite unpleasant. It's one of the reasons I spend so much time sitting on the balcony these days, gazing out to sea.

'I think…' I utter, feeling suddenly nervous. 'I think maybe we should move on.'

'Huh? What do you mean?' Seb asks, a look of alarm on his face.

I realise my heart's beating faster in my chest, my palms beading with sweat.

'We can't live here forever,' I point out, feeling like I've addressed the elephant in the room. 'I'm… I'm not sure I feel like I belong here anymore.'

Seb looks down at the ground. He frowns.

'We still have a bit of time left on our visas, we could go on holiday?' he suggests after a moment, looking back up. 'Go somewhere else for a bit.'

I nod, realising he's dodged the bigger issue of the future of our relationship.

'We may as well explore more of Asia while we're in this part of the world,' he comments.

'Where do you want to go? I ask him.

Seb shrugs. 'Vietnam would be cool. Maybe Thailand,' he suggests.

I shake my head. The last thing I want to do right now is go to Thailand. My future is unclear, and my head is a mess, I definitely don't feel like going to a tourist hotspot, full of beach parties and bars.

'How about Nepal?' Seb suggest, his eyes lighting up.

Nepal is more appealing. I think of the serene lakes, beautiful temples, fluttering bunting. Nepal would probably make a good change. It seems like an interesting place with beautiful scenery and it's not a full-on party destination like some of the other countries in Asia. I picture me and Seb visiting temples or sitting in a little boat on a big still lake between mountains. It could be heavenly and just what I need after battling a stressful legal case.

'Yeah, that might be fun,' I reply, warming to the idea.

Seb smiles enthusiastically. 'That's what we should do then, let's go to Nepal!' he says brightly.

'Okay,' I laugh, amused at how spontaneous he is, how totally willing he is to go with the flow. His adventurous spirit is infectious.

'Let's go to Nepal then.'

'Let's do it!' Seb smiles. He reaches over and takes my hand, lacing his long fingers through mine.

I squeeze his hand and lean in for a kiss.

So our next stop is Nepal. It's not quite what I expected the result of a conversation about our future to be, and the uncertainty is still weighing on my mind, but going to Nepal will be an interesting adventure and it might help. Things have been fun here, but they have been getting a bit stale too. A change of scenery will probably do us both good and it might allow us to put things into perspective. Eventually we'll have to discuss our future, whether it's here or in Kathmandu.

'I can't wait!' Seb enthuses. 'When shall we leave?'

2 CHAPTER TWO

I know I shouldn't be going anywhere near the ashram, but my closest friend in India is eight months pregnant and she can barely move. I met Meera when I first arrived at the ashram since she runs the guesthouse I was staying at and while I think she found me and my London ways a bit annoying to begin with, we soon hit it off. Meera was convinced Seb and I would get together before we even realised it ourselves. She's a great person and I couldn't be happier for her that she's starting a family. She's married to this shy retiring American guy called Fred. He used to work on Wall Street but had a burn out and ended up in India trying to clear his head, and then he never went home. They've been together for years and run their guesthouse together too. They've been trying for a baby for a while. Meera didn't tell anyone she was pregnant, keeping it a secret for quite a long time, and to be honest, I thought she'd just taken her penchant for buttery parathas a bit too far, but then she revealed she's five months pregnant. Since then, she's been taking it easy, hosting fewer guests than usual and spending time in the guesthouse garden, sunbathing and relaxing, while her husband takes care of pretty much everything else. Her baby bump is massive. She insists she's not having twins but I have my doubts. We haven't been seeing as much of each other since I moved out of the guesthouse and became busy with my case, but we still try to catch up every couple of weeks.

'As if anyone in the ashram could remove you by force,' Meera laughed, when I told her about the letter over the phone the other day.

She had a point. Most of the ashram devotees are waif-like airy fairy hippy types who couldn't be any less forceful.

I still feel a bit nervous to be venturing back to the ashram though, but I couldn't exactly ask Meera to come to me in her state. I've adopted a disguise, donning big dark sunglasses and a headscarf. I look a bit odd, but a lot of the devotees look a bit odd, so I should probably blend in.

As I approach the ashram, there's a security guard sitting at the entrance. I don't remember the ashram having security guards before. Is this a new measure? To deter the likes of me?! If it is, it isn't exactly working very well. The guard is sitting on a chair soaking up the sun, reading the newspaper while smoking a cigarette. He barely looks up as I walk past him and head inside.

I let out a sigh of relief as I wander down one of the ashram's dusty winding terracotta paths, dappled with light. The ashram is a soothing place, calm and ambient. It doesn't allow cars and so there are none of the sounds of car horns, angry rickshaw drivers and screeching engines that I've become so used to in the city. Pondicherry is always bustling with activity, full of locals as well as tourists. There are hagglers, beggars, tourists, drunks, wayward hippies and everyday people going about their lives, whereas the ashram is an enclave of spirituality. It's full of hippies and the guru's devotees, who tend to speak in hushed tones and have a generally muted vibe about them. Everyone here is devoted to their spiritual journey and the atmosphere is very subdued with devotees wandering peacefully between yoga classes and meditation sessions. Unlike the village, which is a chaotic mish-mash of flats, houses, shacks and shops, the ashram is full of neat gardens, pretty guesthouses and gorgeous temples for meditation. Even though I'm banned, I feel myself relax immediately as I wander down its sunny paths, the atmosphere so quiet I can hear the birds chirping in the branches overhead.

I pass a couple of devotees, wearing white robes, and I instantly lower my head, hoping they don't recognise me, but they barely look my way, they just chat quietly amongst themselves, oblivious to me walking past.

I approach Meera's guesthouse and head inside, feeling a rush of affection at being back in this familiar place. The guesthouse where I found myself after a really difficult break-up. The guesthouse where Seb and I met. The guesthouse where we fell in love.

I spot Meera sitting at a picnic table in the guesthouse garden, working on her laptop.

She looks up as I approach, her eyes lighting up.

'Hey!' she says.

I pull off my sunglasses.

'Hey!' I reply, rushing up to her and giving her a massive hug.

'Wow, you're huge!' I comment, taking in her bump, which is even bigger than I remember.

'I know, right?!' Meera laughs.

It must have been three weeks since we last saw each other. Things got incredibly busy work-wise as I neared the end of my case, and Meera's bump looks like it's practically doubled in size in that time.

'I cannot wait for this kid to come out! I've gone from feeling terrified of birth to just wanting to get it over and done with,' Meera says.

'Are you sure it's just one kid in there? And not twins? Triplets?' I ask, sitting down opposite her.

'Don't say that!' Meera comments, shaking her head.

I grin, still unable to quite accept that a bump that big could only be home to one baby.

'So you're really not nervous?' I ask.

'I am, but I'm sick of being like this more,' Meera says,

gesturing at her belly and pulling a face.

She does look tired and a bit stressed, her brow beading in the heat. She wipes the sweat from her forehead with the back of her hand.

'Oh, sorry, I should get you a drink,' she says. 'Baby brain!'

'Don't be silly, I'll get them,' I say, jumping up and heading to the guesthouse kitchen, where I used to prepare my meals every day.

I bring back a jug of water and two glasses.

'There's some barfi in the fridge,' Meera comments.

'Ohh!'

I head back to the kitchen and retrieve a small box of the delicious milky sweet.

I hand Meera the box as I sit back down. She opens it, placing it on the table between us. The squares of barfi are dusted with desiccated coconut and pistachios. They look mouth-wateringly delicious. I hadn't tried barfi before I came to India, but now I love it. It's the most delicious indulgence imaginable. There are loads of Indian foods that I now wonder how I ever lived without, from buttery paratha flatbreads to dosa rice pancakes, and even just simple things like chai.

Meera pushes her laptop aside and tucks into the barfi, before pushing the box towards me. I help myself to a piece. It's melt-in-your-mouth good.

'Delicious!' I comment.

'I've been eating this stuff non-stop. I blame my pregnancy!' Meera grins. 'Fred keeps buying it because of my cravings. It's one of the plus points of being pregnant!'

'Mmm, definitely,' I reply, reaching for another piece of barfi.

Meera might be getting sick of being pregnant, but I know how excited she is to be a mum. She told me she's dreamt of being a mother ever since she was a little girl. Unlike her, I've never really given having children much thought, even though for a long time, I lived my life according to a Life List. Back when I was a teenager, before I left home for university, I made a list of all the things I wanted to achieve in life, with everything carefully plotted out on a timeline, from scoring a place at a good university at 18, to getting a good job in law by 22, to being in a steady relationship by 26 and getting married by 30. I managed to tick off all the goals on my Life List apart from marriage. As I approached my 31st birthday, I was so desperate to stick to my Life List that I convinced myself my boyfriend Paul was going to propose. I was so obsessed with the idea that I somehow lost sight of the fact that Paul and I weren't as close as we used to be and weren't even compatible. We went out for dinner in London one evening, to the restaurant where we had our first date, and I was convinced Paul was planning to pop the question, but instead he told me he was going to India to find himself and that we were over. I was so distraught that I decided to follow him to India and win him back, except when I got here and rocked up at the ashram, where he was staying, I ended up realising that I was lost too, and that I needed to find myself. In the end, I tore up my Life List and started going with the flow a bit more. Since then, I haven't given much thought to marriage or kids. I'd like both to happen at some point, but I've learnt from past experience that you can't force such things.

Meera tells me about her pregnancy cravings and the weird foods she's been eating, everything from fresh chillies to gorging on Gulab Jamun. As she talks, I nibble on barfi.

'So, what's up with you then?' she asks. 'How's Seb?'

'Oh, he's good,' I reply, smiling.

Meera smiles, a little smugly. I think she feels like Cupid when it comes to me and Seb. She nudged us towards each other on a few occasions at around the time we got together.

Meera smiles conspiratorially.

'You two are so perfect together,' she comments.

'I know!' I admit. 'He's amazing. We've had such an incredible time here, but I don't know where it's going, you know. Seb seems to just want to keep on taking each day as it comes, living in the moment, you know what he's like!'

Meera laughs. 'Yep!'

'But my case is over now. My visa's going to run out soon and then what? I don't know what the future holds for us.'

'Haven't you spoken about this?' Meera asks, looking perplexed.

I shake my head. 'Not really. I was so busy with the case that honestly, I just didn't have the mental capacity to think about that too. Seb hasn't brought it up. He must think about it, I think…' I trail off, thinking of Seb and his meditation, his spirituality, how much he appreciates the little things in life, from a beautiful butterfly landing on the balcony to a gorgeous sunset. Sometimes I wonder how much he does thinks beyond the here and now.

'Actually, I don't know if he does think about it,' I comment.

'You need to talk to him,' Meera insists, a serious look in her eyes. 'You're going to have to talk about it sooner or later.'

'Well, I tried to…' I tell Meera about my attempt to broach the subject with Seb and how he didn't seem to want to discuss our future beyond more than just a couple of weeks ahead. I start offloading about my confusion – how I'm beginning to miss home, but how I love Seb and our relationship and don't want to rock the boat prematurely. How I'm worried that if I get serious about our future, Seb might just run a mile.

'Seb loves you,' Meera insists.

'I know he does, but he's also a free spirit,' I remind her. 'And I don't know if he'd like London.'

'Hmm…' Meera murmurs.

Meera is the kind of person who believes there are no real barriers to true love, probably because of her unusual relationship with Fred since he abandoned his life in the US for her in India. But I don't think she realises that making huge sacrifice like that is pretty rare.

'Seb suggested a trip to Nepal,' I tell her.

'Nepal?' Meera echoes, surprised.

'Yeah!' I reply, shrugging.

'For how long?'

'Just a couple of weeks,' I reach for another piece of barfi. 'He thinks a change of scenery would do us good.'

Meera nods. 'He's probably right actually. It might be good for you. Sometimes you just have to go with the flow, trust in the universe and see where it takes you,' she says, sounding like a total hippy.

Meera is a lot more grounded than a lot of the airy-fairy types here who tend to trot out spiritual mumbo-jumbo like they've been staring at motivational quotes on Instagram's #positivevibes for too long. But even though Meera isn't really like that, she still has her moments.

'I think a trip to Nepal might help,' she continues. 'It'll get you out of your comfort zone, give you a new challenge. It will test you as a couple. I mean Everest is either going to make or break you, right? At least after this trip, you'll know whether or not Seb is the right person for you.'

'I hadn't thought of it like that,' I admit.

'I think this trip will be good for you two,' Meera says, smiling, reaching for another piece of barfi too. We've demolished two thirds of the pack.

'When Fred and I first got together, he wanted me to go to New York with him to visit his family. I was terrified. I'd never left India before. I'd hardly even left the ashram, but it was important to him to introduce me to his parents and his brother so I decided to just go for it. I was so nervous and tense, but in the end, I loved it. Fred's parents were so kind and welcoming and we got on so well. It made me feel even more confident that he was the right guy for me. That trip brought us so much closer together,' Meera recounts, smiling to herself at the memory. 'And New York! New York was incredible!'

Her eyes sparkle.

I nod, feeling more comforted. Nepal probably is the right

thing to do. It will probably bring us closer together. I just need to be strong.

Meera has such an effortless ability to put things into perspective and yet I feel another wave of sadness.

'What's up?' she asks, clocking the look on my face.

'I was just thinking, you're totally right. It is time for me and Seb to leave India and it will be amazing, it's probably just what we need, and yet I'm going to miss this place so much. And you.'

I smile sadly at her. She's been such a good friend to me that it's going to be really hard to say goodbye.

'Oh…' Meera smile sadly back at me. 'I'm going to miss you too.'

She reaches over and takes my hand. 'But we'll always have the phone, Facebook, WhatsApp. And we can visit each other, right?'

'Definitely,' I reply.

She's right. Just because my time spent living in India might be coming to an end, it doesn't mean I'm never going to spend time here again. There are so many parts of the country that I haven't visited. I've not even seen the Taj Mahal.

I squeeze Meera's hand and gaze into her warm, familiar eyes when suddenly heavy footsteps interrupt our moment.

'Rachel Watson!' A man says.

He's dressed in uniform and I realise it's the security guard who was smoking and reading the paper as I walked into the ashram.

I look at Meera, alarmed. She looks as shocked as me.

'You're not allowed to be here,' the man says, standing next to our table, glowering at me.

I try to think of a reason as to why I'm here, but the truth is I'm here because I wanted to chat with my friend about my love life. It doesn't exactly count as extenuating circumstances.

'You need to leave immediately!' The man insists, raising his voice.

'Okay, okay!' I reply, getting up.

'Oh, come on,' Meera sighs, rolling her eyes. 'She's not doing anything wrong.'

'She's banned,' the man states, while eyeballing me.

I find myself wondering again if he's been employed specifically to keep me out of the ashram. I wouldn't put it past Guru Hridaya.

'You need to get out of here,' the guard spits.

'I'm going,' I grumble.

'No,' Meera protests. 'You're my guest and this is my property.'

She shoots the guard a look.

Technically, she owns the guesthouse, but legally, the ashram land is owned by Guru Hridaya and if I'm banned from the ashram, I'm pretty sure that includes her guesthouse. But I don't point that out. I'm touched, instead, by how much she's willing to stand up for me.

'No. She must leave,' the guard barks.

His eyes are blazing. He looks really annoyed and it's clear that he takes his job very seriously.

'You must leave immediately,' he says. 'Or I will remove you.'

'I'm leaving! I'm leaving!' I reply, rolling my eyes while reluctantly getting up.

Meera carries on arguing with the guard. He's getting increasingly incensed and before I know it, he's grabbed me, gripping my arms and he's frog-marching me away from her.

'Oh my God!' Meera utters, clasping her hand over her mouth. 'I can't believe this, let go of her.'

She tries to get up and I'm worried she's going to come after us and start trying to wrestle me free from the guard.

'Meera, sit down!' I call out insistently. 'Just leave it! You're too pregnant.'

Meera glances down at her enormous belly, almost as though she'd forgotten it was there. She rolls her eyes and sits back down, realising she's in no fit state to take on this guard.

'I'll call you,' I call out over my shoulder as the guard frog-marches me away.

'Okay. There was something I was going to ask you,' Meera calls back, looking pained and desperate.

Registering her expression, I turn back to the guard, giving him my most searching look.

'Please, can I just have five minutes with my friend?' I ask, 'Five minute and then I'll go,' I implore him, trying to find some compassion in him.

'No. You are BANNED!' The guard barks, even more incensed than before.

'Let's talk later, Meera,' I say, pulling a face behind the guard as he turns his head.

Meera shakes her head.

'I'm going to complain about this!' she shouts after the guard.

But he doesn't respond. He doesn't seem bothered at all. He just carries on frog-marching me down the path out of the guesthouse.

I look over my shoulder at Meera, feeling sad and disappointed that this is probably one of the last times I'll see her before leaving India and here I am, being escorted off the premises. She looks just as cut up as me. But the guard doesn't care, he just marches me away.

I wave at Meera and she waves back as he marches me out of the guesthouse garden and out of sight.

He grips me as he marches me along the path leading out of the ashram. He's breathing heavily and his hands are sweaty against my arms.

'You can let go of me,' I tell him.

'No,' he replies simply.

I can't tell whether his English is bad or if he's just being rude.

He grips me tightly and carries on marching me out of the ashram like I'm a criminal. I consider protesting again, but it occurs to me that he might have handcuffs or connections to the local police. The last thing I want is to provoke him to the point that he handcuffs me or gets me into trouble with the law.

I give in, allowing him to march me out of the ashram.

A few of the devotees passing by spot what's happening and start nudging each other, pointing. A couple of them hold their phones up and start snapping away, clearly amused.

'Oh my God,' I grumble, lowering my head, not wanting to be photographed.

I realise I left my sunglasses and headscarf on the picnic table at Meera's. I don't even have my disguise with me. Great.

I keep my head down but they carry on snapping away as the guard marches me to the exit. We walk out.

'You can let go of me now,' I tell him.

Finally, he let's go.

'You are banned. Do not come here again,' he spits, looking furious.

'I know. I got the message,' I huff, rolling my eyes.

Feeling angry and humiliated, I hurry back to the flat.

3 CHAPTER THREE

I sit on the balcony of the flat sipping coffee, soaking in the morning sunshine. I'm scrolling on Facebook and Twitter, seeing what my friends and family back home are up to. My best friend, Priya, has posted a scanned polaroid picture from her wedding in Vegas. It's a shot of her and her entrepreneur husband Rene smiling, looking so happy, in front of a gaudy casino, holding up their hands to show their wedding rings. It's a gorgeous shot and they look so completely overjoyed, their eyes sparkling. I hit like and write a comment telling them how much I love the picture and how happy I am for them. I was so surprised when Priya told me a few months ago that she and her boyfriend were eloping to Vegas to get married. Priya and I met on the first day at our law firm back in London. We were both on our firm's graduate scheme and we've stuck by each other over the years, both of us rising up to partner level. Priya is one of the most driven, ambitious people I know. Like I used to with my Life List, she sets herself goals and targets that she's always striving to achieve. I knew getting married was one of her goals, but I'd always imagined that she would want a traditional wedding. Yet she said I'd inspired her with my adventurous spirit through my India trip and she decided to be a bit more adventurous and spontaneous too. Rather than having a big white wedding, she and Rene secretly booked flights to Vegas and got married at a retro chapel on the Strip. She said it was the most romantic way they could have possibly got married because it was just about them. It was as intimate as it gets. Their joy radiates from the picture.

I hear the front door opening, distracting me from my thoughts.

Seb has come back from his morning run. He usually sets off before I wake up and jogs around the village or along the beach.

'Hey,' he says, coming onto the balcony, sweat dripping off him.

It's boiling and I don't know how he manages to run in the heat. I feel like I'm melting half the time, but nothing gets between Seb and exercise.

'Hey,' I reply a little surprised that he's come out onto the balcony since normally he jumps straight in the shower.

He sits down next to me, frowning. He's holding a newspaper.

'What's up?' I ask.

Seb takes a deep breath.

'So I was running past the newsagents and umm...' He frowns, a squirming expression on his face.

'What?' I reply, baffled.

I reach for the paper, worried that something bad has happened in the community. A murder? A rape? An impending natural disaster?

'What's up?' I ask.

Seb glances down at the paper.

'It's... Err...' he stammers.

'What's going on?' I ask.

I reach for the paper. Seb lets me have it. I unroll it on my lap and scan the front page. It's emblazoned with the headline: 'Woman who sued guru breaks ashram ban', accompanied by an unflattering photo of me being frog-marched out of the ashram.

'Oh my God,' I utter, scanning the article.

A British lawyer who took on Guru Hridaya in a legal challenge over tax evasion was escorted off the ashram premises after breaking a ban forbidding her from entering the site.

An ashram security guard had to remove Rachel Watson, 31, who works for London law firm Pearson & Co, after she trespassed on Tuesday afternoon.

The incident occurred just days after Miss Watson was informed of her formal ban from the site.

The ban comes after the tax lawyer successfully sued Guru Hridaya for tax evasion.

The article goes on to include details about the case and a quote from the security guard stating that if I attempt to enter the ashram again, I 'may face arrest'.

'Oh God! They're talking about arresting me!' I gawp.

Seb pulls a face. 'Yeah, you should probably avoid the ashram from now on.'

'And these pictures…' I take a closer look at the photos accompanying the article.

One of the devotees who was snapping my picture must have sent them to the local paper. I look awful in them, totally stressed out. In one shot I'm scowling angrily at the guard. They've clearly chosen the worst picture they had.

'This is *so* embarrassing,' I grumble.

'You really are a local celebrity,' Seb comments, with a half-smile.

I roll my eyes.

'I'm not sure I'm cut out for the celebrity life,' I sigh, pushing the paper away. I look out to the sea, lapping at the shore.

'I think we should go to Nepal as soon as possible!' I comment.

Seb nods as though he's been expecting my reaction.

'I'll have a shower and start looking into flights,' he says.

'Ok great,' I reply. 'And we need to let Raj know.'

Raj is our landlord. Fortunately, we rent our flat on a month-by-month basis so it's pretty easy for us to up sticks and leave.

'Yeah,' Seb replies.

I glance back down at the article.

'Honestly!' I tut.

'Are you sure you don't want to ride on the wave of fame?' Seb teases.

'No, I think I'm good!' I reply.

Seb laughs and heads off to go and have a shower.

I look back at my phone and a horrible thought occurs to me. What if the article is online? I quickly google it and I'm relieved to find that it's not. I breathe a sigh of relief and write a status update on Facebook.

'So guys, it looks like I'm leaving India and heading to Nepal' I add a couple of exclamation marks and the likes start pouring in.

4 CHAPTER FOUR

I decide to spend the day sunbathing on the beach to relax after the drama of the article. After lazing around reading a book and soaking up some sun, I go for a walk along the beach before heading back home.

The moment I get into the flat, Seb comes bounding up to me like a puppy.

'I have a surprise for you!' he says, grinning, before kissing me.

'Oh God, what?' I groan. 'I think I've had enough surprises for the moment.'

'No, this is a *good* surprise!' Seb insists.

I raise an eyebrow. 'Really?' I reply sceptically as I kick off my sandals.

We wander into the kitchen.

'Definitely!' Seb insists. 'I found tickets to Nepal, leaving this weekend. They're so cheap!'

'Oh, okay… This weekend, that's so soon,' I comment, feeling taken aback as I take a bottle of water from the fridge.

I knew we were going to leave at some point, but this weekend feels pretty sudden. It's only Wednesday.

'Well, they were cheap and we're planning to leave soon, aren't we,' Seb says.

'How cheap?' I ask.

'Two hundred pounds, for both of us!' Seb enthuses.

'Wow, that is cheap,' I reply, taking a sip of my water.

'But that's not the surprise,' Seb comments.

'What is the surprise then?' I ask.

'It's in the bedroom,' he says.

'Ooohh!' I reply, brightening up. I give him a cheeky wink.

Seb laughs. 'It's not that kind of surprise.'

'What is it then?' I ask curiously as he leads me into the bedroom, where I see the bed is covered in an array of... hiking equipment.

Hiking boots, compasses, maps, mosquito repellent, trekking poles, sun cream, even a whistle.

It's not quite the sexy surprise I'd been hoping for.

'Oh. Wow!' I reply, taking it all in, feeling a bit daunted.

Compasses? Am I Crocodile Dundee all of a sudden? And those hiking boots. They're so chunky and enormous. Totally hideous. Even the water flask looks like a brick.

'Seb, what is all this for?' I ask.

'Umm... Everest, obviously!' Seb points out.

'Everest?! What?' I balk.

'Yeah! Why do you seem so shocked?' Seb regards me, wide eyed.

'Everest! That's for, like, seasoned hikers. You know, proper explorers. We can't climb *Everest*!' I utter, feeling uneasy.

'Of course, we can,' Seb insists. 'We have to! We can't go to Nepal and not climb Everest!' Seb laughs. 'That would be like coming to India and not going to a temple or going to France and not trying snails.'

'But Seb!' I take in all the supplies he's bought, which include mosquito repellent and leech repellent.

I pick up the spray in horror.

'Leech repellent?' I gawp.

'Yeah, apparently it's essential. There are loads of leeches on the Everest trail,' Seb tells me matter-of-factly.

I look at the label on the spray can. *This fast-acting spray provides advanced protection against blood-sucking leeches.*

'Blood-sucking leeches! Seb?!' I groan, feeling exasperated. It's like he thinks leeches are no big deal. And climbing Everest is no biggie either.

'You'll thank me later!' Seb comments, eyeing the leech spray in my hand.

'Seb! Leeches? Really?'

'Yeah, surely you're used to annoying insects by now?' he says.

There are definitely a lot more insects over here than there are back home – mosquitos, cockroaches, tropical spiders, but there aren't *leeches*. Blood-sucking leeches are a whole other league.

I slump onto the bed, the leech spray in my hands.

'I thought you'd be excited!' Seb says, looking a bit forlorn as he sits down next to me.

'I was excited to go to Nepal, but I thought we'd do tourist stuff, go to temples, visit lakes, go to markets, eat momos. I didn't think we'd hike up *Everest*!' I point out.

'But it's Everest!' Seb protests, looking at me with a searching gaze. 'We can't miss out on Everest.'

He's clearly really excited about this. He's bought everything from a compass to leech repellant for goodness sake. He looks genuinely shocked and a little hurt by my lack of enthusiasm and I can't help feeling a little bit guilty. He's made a load of compromises for me recently. He was happy in the ashram, but he moved out here with me because of the legal case. He hardly ever goes back to the ashram these days since I've been banned. He doesn't want to make me feel left out or ostracized but I know he loves that place despite Guru Hridaya's corruption. I know he misses it and all the friends he had there who he used to see daily. His sacrifices haven't gone unnoticed. It probably is about time I do something for Seb even if that means donning a pair of gigantic, hideous hiking boots.

'Don't you need to train to climb Everest though?' I ask.

'No, not for base camp. We not going to reach the summit! You have to train for months to do that. Is that what you thought I was thinking?'

I nod.

Seb laughs. 'No, just base camp. It's a fourteen-day trek. It's totally safe. You don't get too high up the mountains. It's a pretty gentle hike. You don't have to train, pretty much anyone can do it,' Seb explains, eagerly.

I spot sleeping bags on the bed.

'Are we going to camp? On Everest?' I ask, shocked.

'No! I just bought them because they were cheap and I've heard that the guesthouses on Everest can be a bit basic,' Seb explains.

'Right,' I reply, looking at our nice silk bedspread underneath the sleeping bags and the lovely cushions that adorn our bed. They're hand-embroidered and I bought them from the ashram gift shop when I first arrived here, back when I was still obsessed with home furnishings. I'll probably have to leave them behind or five them to Meera. I can't exactly be lugging a ton of cushions up Everest. I feel a little twinge of sadness yet again at the thought of moving on, even though I know it's time.

I notice my Ted Baker suitcase, which I rocked up to India with is by the side of the bed.

'Oh, you got that down,' I comment, gesturing at it. It had been on top of the wardrobe.

'Yeah, I was wondering what you wanted to do with it. It's probably not ideal for our trek,' Seb comments.

'No, it's probably not!' I admit.

'I remember the first time I saw you, trying to get that suitcase up to your treehouse,' Seb remarks.

I laugh.

The first time Seb ever spoke to me was to offer to help me with my case when he saw me trying and failing to carry it up a ladder to my treehouse. I hadn't realised that my trip to India and my accommodation was a lot more suited to backpackers than suitcasers. My pink shiny case with its jewelled pattern is more the kind of thing you'd take on a holiday to Marbella than bring on a trip to an ashram in India. I'd packed it full of the most ridiculous items as well, things I didn't realise were totally unsuited to ashram life, like a pair of purple suede Prada wedges, hair straighteners and even fake tan.

'What's up?' Seb asks. 'Do you really not want to go?'

I realise I must have been looking a bit down. Really, I was just feeling wistful about all the good times I've had here in India.

'No, I do, I'm just a little sad to leave I guess, even though I know we have to eventually,' I admit, feeling a lump form instantly in my throat.

Despite a corrupt guru, annoying hippies, horrible squatty toilets, mosquitoes and getting banned from the ashram, there's still so much I'm going to miss about this place. I'm going to miss the birdsong in the mornings, the open-hearted people, the lush palm trees, the sunshine, the sound of the sea, the delicious food.

'I guess we can't stay here forever,' I comment.

'I'm going to miss it too.' Seb wraps his arms around me and pulls me close. 'But it's going to be okay,' he assures me, giving my shoulder a squeeze. 'You said it yourself, we need to move on. You don't want to be a local celebrity, banned from the ashram, being frog-marched out.'

'Yeah, I know,' I admit.

'We're going to be okay wherever we go,' Seb assures me, kissing me on the forehead. 'The most important thing is that we have each other.'

I smile. He's right, I just hope we have each other for a long time, because the last thing I want is to uproot from this relationship.

Seb carries on bundling the hiking gear into his backpack as I sit on the edge of the bed watching him. I look around at our room.

It's huge, the kind of large room that would cost an absolute fortune in London. It has tall bay windows and when our landlord, Raj, first showed it to us, I fell in love with it instantly. Before I came to India, I was obsessed with home furnishings. And when I say obsessed I mean *obsessed*. I had an Instagram account dedicated to the makeover and décor of the house I shared with my ex, Paul. I spent every weekend at IKEA or Homebase picking up lamps, coffee tables, paint samples, you name it. My house had become my main focus in life to the point that I hadn't even realised my relationship was falling apart. My ex, Paul, has been living in our house alone since we broke up and I decided to stay in India. He said he'd move out when I was ready to come back since I agreed to buy him out of the mortgage. I don't know whether he's still spending time on decorating it I doubt it since apparently I bored him silly with all that stuff and he certainly hasn't been updating the Instagram account. I miss my London house, but I'm going to miss this flat too.

I glance over at Seb who is packing blister ointment into his bag.

5 CHAPTER FIVE

I think I had a lump in my throat for two full days from Friday to
Saturday as we packed for our trip, cleaned out the flat and said
goodbye to friends we've made. It was the most heart-wrenching
experience ever and was made even more intense by Meera going
into labour. We were due to say goodbye at her uncle's café
around the corner from the ashram, meeting for lunch on Saturday
just before we were due to set off, but she called me in the
morning, groaning and barely coherent, saying she was having
contractions and going into early labour. I left my Ted Baker
suitcase full of cushions and a few other bits and pieces, as well as
a note, with a mutual friend and sent her encouraging text
messages as she was rushed into the ward, but we didn't get a
chance to say goodbye properly. Maybe it's for the best since it
would have been so emotional. At least this way, I know I'll have
to come back soon, not only to properly see Meera again but to
meet her child. Or children. I haven't heard yet if I'm right and
she's having twins. By the time she arrived at the hospital and was
taken to the maternity ward, Seb and I were getting onto the plane
to Nepal. It's been so dramatic, and I found myself bursting into
tears like a child as the plane took off from the airport, the sadness
of leaving India and people who mean so much to me, feeling
extremely raw. But at least I have Seb by my side. He understood
and he's been lovely about it, holding my hand and ordering me

double G&T's to take the edge off.

It's dark by the time our plane begins its descent towards Nepal. I've had a nap, and I feel a bit better now. I'm sad about leaving India, and it's incredibly frustrating to not have wifi up here to check in on Meera, but never mind. I'm going to try to be positive and see Nepal as a new adventure, an opportunity for new experiences, with new places to see, new people to meet and new food to try. I think about what Priya - my best friend back home - said before I set off to India: 'If you smile at India, India smiles back'. I found her saying a little funny at the time but once I got to India, it made sense. People respond to your vibes and your attitude in India and if you have good 'energy' things tend to go your way a lot more. If you have a good attitude then you don't mind as much that the trains and buses always run late, you take the chaotic driving in your stride, you roll with the strange spiritual stuff. But Priya's saying can apply to anywhere really. If I arrive in Nepal feeling miserable, full of dread about climbing Everest and not really wanting to be there then I'm going to have a rubbish time.

I'm tired though and I am looking forward to getting to the hotel. I need to sleep and I'm also really hungry. Seb and I may have booked budget flights, but I didn't realise they were so budget that we wouldn't even get fed aside from a few bags of peanuts and a cup of tea. I haven't eaten properly for hours and I'm famished.

Our plane begins plunging down to the runway. I brace myself as my stomach flips and my ears pop. Seb and I exchange a look, neither of us particularly enjoying the sensation. Seb has a book open on his lap that he's been completely gripped by, churning through it during the flight. It's a memoir of a guy who climbed Everest. He read out a few passages to me, about feats of bravery and moments of extreme difficulty this explorer overcame during his expedition. Everything that could have gone wrong during this guy's expedition went wrong. From fierce arctic winds, to bites by deadly spiders, to wind-blasted tents on perilous cliff-faces. It's like the hiker's version of a misery memoir and is definitely not whetting my appetite for this hike, but the more life-threatening this guy's story gets, the more energized Seb seems to become about our base camp trek. I'm starting to worry he has a death wish, even though he keeps telling me that our trip is going to be nothing like this guy's since we're only trekking around base camp and we're not actually scaling Everest, but even so…

By the time our plane finally lands, I'm starving. I'm craving a Burger King or a Costa Coffee like the ones I always pick up at Heathrow back in England. It's thoughts like this that make me realise how homesick I'm beginning to get. I've barely thought about the shops back home for months, but now little thoughts like that are creeping back. The plane lands and Seb and I make our way towards the customs desk.

There's a huge queue, but I get my phone out and try to connect to WiFi, hoping there's a signal in the airport. I'm desperate to have an update from Meera. Fortunately, a few bars of WiFi signal appear on an open network. I'm in luck!

I connect and open WhatsApp, hoping she or her husband Fred will have got in touch while we've been on the plane.

There's a message from Fred.

Fred: You were right! Meera's having twins! She's just delivered our first. A little boy, 6lb! He's gorgeous!

'Oh my god!' I squeal. 'Meera's having twins!'

A few other travellers look my way, alarmed by my excited shrieks after a long late-night flight. Seb is just as thrilled as I am. He's always got on well with Meera.

'Did they send a pic?' he asks.

'No, not yet,' I reply.

I fire back a message telling them how happy we are for them.

'I can't wait to see pictures!' I enthuse.

'They'll be adorable. I wonder if it'll be two boys or two

girls?' Seb muses.

'Meera really didn't think it was twins. She thought she just had some mammoth baby growing in there,' I comment.

Seb laughs.

'I hope Meera's doing okay,' I add, thinking about how stressful it must be to have to go through birth not once, but twice.

I send another message to Fred to ask how she is.

We reach the end of the customs queue and show our passports. We're given our traveller's visas and then we go to collect our bags, before walking through the airport towards the exit. It's 2am and all the shops and restaurants are closed. My stomach is rumbling with hunger, churning so much that it's almost painful.

'Oh my God,' I grumble to Seb. 'I'm starving.'

We head towards the taxi rank.

'We might be able to pick something up in Kathmandu,' Seb suggests.

Something catches my eye in the distance. It looks like a food cart.

'What's that?' I utter, pointing towards it.

'Let's go check it out!' Seb suggests brightly.

Hungry and sagging under the weight of our backpacks, we walk towards the cart.

As we approach, I see it's just a man selling nothing but scrawny-looking bird carcasses, rotating over a spit, its coals glowing in the darkness. I look around to see if there's something else to go with the chicken, or pheasant, or whatever type of bird it is, but no, it appears to be just emaciated-looking birds.

'What is this?' Seb asks the man, pointing at one of the scrawny-looking carcasses.

'Chicken,' the man replies.

I eye the chickens warily. They look half the size of regular chickens. Unless they're just malnourished baby chicks. The spit they're roasting on doesn't look particularly clean. My mouth isn't exactly watering and yet I am starving, and my stomach is rumbling in spite of myself at the smell of them roasting.

I shrug. 'I'm up for it,' I tell Seb.

He raises his eyebrows, surprised, but I don't back down.

'Okay!' He shrugs back.

We ask the man for two.

He pulls two carcasses off the spit with a fork and then begins pulling scraps of meat off the bones with his bare hands. I pull a face at Seb, who looks equally uneasy. Some of the meat is a little pink. The man hands us two paper plates with nothing but chicken meat on each.

Seb pays the man and thanks him in Nepalese.

We walk away. Once we're out of earshot, I turn to Seb.

'Do you think this is safe to eat?' I ask, eyeing the meat uneasily.

'Maybe if we eat the whiter bits it'll be okay,' Seb comments.

'I don't know…' I murmur. 'Maybe we should just get something in Kathmandu after all.'

'I reckon it'll be fine,' Seb insists, eyeing his plate. 'It doesn't look that bad.'

'Hmmm…' I murmur.

Seb starts shoveling the chicken into his mouth with his fingers.

'Mmm, it's actually really nice,' he says.

I feel torn between wariness and hunger, but as I watch Seb demolish his plate, I can't resist trying a little bit of my chicken too. I pick up some white-looking breast meat and pop it into my mouth, trying not to think of the man touching it with his bare hands or the pinkness of the flesh. Seb's right, it is quite nice. It's salty and lightly spiced. I pop another piece into my mouth, and before I know it, I've scoffed the whole lot.

'That was good,' I reply, feeling full and satisfied.

'Delicious,' Seb comments.

I laugh. 'Don't know if I'd go that far!'

'Yeah, maybe not quite,' Seb replies, laughing.

We throw our plates in a nearby bin and get a taxi to our hotel in Kathmandu. I think about the first day I arrived in India, touching down at Bangalore Airport. I got into a taxi with a driver who wouldn't stop talking and was barely concentrating on the road. In fact, he was so erratic that he crashed into a barrier at the side of the road. Fortunately, we choose a better driver here though. After loading up the boot with our bags, our driver makes his way smoothly to Kathmandu. Sitting together on the backseat, I rest my head on Seb's shoulder. As we near the city, I lift my head to look out of the window. It's dark outside and there aren't many streetlamps. The moon is full and I gaze upwards, taking in tall electricity pylons with looping wires crisscrossing between them. The road is lined with tiny shops with shutters that open onto the street. I spot a few homeless people huddled in walkways. We pull onto a different road, this one populated by hotels, taller, more imposing buildings. We arrive outside our hotel, even though the impression I gained from its website is that it's not really a hotel and more of a hostel, aimed at travellers like ourselves - backpackers doing trips across Asia and embarking on Everest missions. Seb thought it would be a good place to stay because its website was full of pictures of Everest and hiking information. I tried to be enthusiastic but really, I could kill for a nice 5-star hotel with a spa or pool. Maybe I should have suggested it, but I know that we're kind of on a budget and I thought I'd be okay with somewhere cheap, but right now, tired and a bit down, I'd kill for somewhere a little bit luxurious to stay.

Our driver pulls up outside. We pay and get out, collecting our bags from the boot, and then head towards the hotel. It looks closed, even though its sign is emblazoned in bright electric letters that flicker slightly in the darkness. Its large black doors are shut and Seb and I exchange a worried look before knocking on the door. At first, we hear nothing. We knock again, a bit harder this time. A man opens the door, rubbing the sleep from his eyes. He's dressed in a shirt and jeans, but they're crumpled and it's clear he's been sleeping.

'Hi,' he says, gesturing for us to come inside.

'Namaste,' I say, greeting him in Nepali. Seb chimes in.

'Namaste,' he replies, nodding curtly.

The hallway is wide, lined with stone tiles. A TV, mounted to the wall, plays a soap opera in Nepalese.

Yawning and avoiding eye contact, the man walks over to the reception desk.

'Passports,' he says, boredly.

Seb and I hand him our passports.

The man takes them, makes a note in a book and then dumps a room key on the reception desk.

'Fifth floor, room seventeen,' he says, before yawning again.

He slumps back into his chair and turns his attention to the soap opera on the screen behind us.

'Great, thanks,' I say, a little sarcastically.

Seb and I turn around, contemplating the stairs. We're already exhausted and the idea of lugging our bags up five flights of stairs isn't exactly appealing.

'Lift, there,' the man says, pointing down a corridor branching off from reception where there's a lift.

'Thank you,' Seb replies.

We get into the lift.

'Well, he was friendly,' I comment, rolling my eyes, as I press the button for the fifth floor.

'Yeah, charming,' Seb replies.

A fly buzzes around, caught in a light overhead. The lift is dusty with dirt. I run my finger over the wall, leaving a trace in the film of dirt.

'This place is a bit grubby, isn't it?'

'A bit,' Seb admits, grimacing. 'It'll be fine though. We're only here for a few nights.'

I nod. He's right. I can handle a dusty hotel for a couple of nights. And anyway, this hotel is probably going to feel like luxury compared to the sort of places we'll be sleeping in during our Everest trek.

We reach the fifth floor and cross the hallway to room 17. Seb unlocks it while I linger behind him, bracing myself. He opens the door and flicks on the light.

The first thing my eyes land upon are twin beds on rickety-looking metal frames.

'Twin beds?' I balk.

Seb looks just as stricken as I am.

'I did ask for a double. I guess they didn't understand,' he says.

'Oh God,' I sigh, heaving my bag off my back and onto the dusty marble floor.

Seb does the same. The rest of the room is stark and bare, with just a large fan whirring limply overhead.

'Cosy,' I comment.

Seb laughs weakly. He's the optimist in our relationship but even he looks a little bit put out by our miserable-looking room.

'Oh well, I sigh, flopping down onto the bed.

It creaks under my weight. Suddenly the lights in our room go off.

'What?' I sit up. 'Did you turn it off?'

'No.' Seb flicks the light switch on and off.

'Power outage,' he sighs, slumping onto his bed. 'Apparently they happen all the time here.'

'Great!' I reply.

6 CHAPTER SIX

Seb and I spend the day sight-seeing in Kathmandu. We visited Boudhanath Stupa temple, a stunning Buddhist temple in the heart of the city. With a huge white-washed dome and a gilded golden tower adorned with the eyes of Buddha, the temple makes for a striking site. Seb and I posed for pictures and explored the monument, learning about its history, from how the thirteen plinths of the tapering golden tower represent the thirteen stages a person must pass through before achieving nirvana to how the 14th century monument is said to house a bone of Buddha. We went to an arts and crafts market and bought s few gifts for people back home before taking a stroll up to world heritage site Swayambhunath temple, climbing two hundred steps to reach the holy spot, which was teeming with monkeys, swinging between the trees overhead. After stopping for a delicious thali, we went back to the hotel.

We head to the hotel bar. It's on the roof, with a huge outdoor bar overlooking the city. Seb goes to get us some drinks while I take a seat at one of the tables with the best view. I gaze out over the rooftops of Kathmandu. Apparently, on good day when the sky is clear, you can see Everest in the distance, but today the view of the Himalayas is shrouded in a blanket of cloud. I'm feeling a little light-headed, but it's probably just tiredness and low blood sugar. I haven't eaten since lunch several hours ago. It's growing dark over the city, the sky fading from a warm light to slate grey.

I check my phone to see if the WiFi signal is available up here. It is! I send a few messages to family back home, letting them know I'm safe and well. It occurs to me that maybe I should send a message to Paul to find out what his plans are and when he's planning to move out since I would like to return to London soon. I fire off a message to him, and then my phone starts pinging with messages. Most of them are from Meera.

Meera: Look at my babies!!! I can't believe you were right! Twins! Meet Ajay and Azar! Xxx

She includes a picture of two adorable, tiny little babies, wearing matching white baby grows lying together in a cot. They both have jet black hair and dark brown eyes, taking after Meera rather than Fred. They're so cute.

Seb comes back from the bar carrying two bottles of beer and a few packets of crisps.

'Look at this,' I say, showing him the picture as he hands me a bottle and one of the packets. 'Meera's twins! Ajay and Azar.'

'Oh wow!' Seb gushes, sitting down and examining the picture. 'They're so cute!'

'I know!'

We check out the rest of the pictures Meera's sent and I send her some messages, making sure she's well. She's online and replies, telling us she's still at hospital but that she's doing fine. She says she's tired and that she needs a nap. We promise to catch up soon and I put my phone back in my bag. I take a sip of my beer, relishing to taste of the cool light beer. I tear open the bag of crisps.

Seb sits down opposite and looks out across the city. We start chatting about our Everest plans and how we're going to make our way to base camp, which is 150 miles away.

'Hey, are you doing Everest too?' An American guy sitting on a nearby table asks.

I hadn't noticed him before, but he's a big guy, clearly works out, with bulging biceps on show under a loose vest. He regards us with bright, keen and friendly eyes. His head is shaved but there's a bit of regrowth. He has dark brown hair that matches his brown eyes and there are tattoos on his chest, creeping out from under his vest. I spot the tip of what looks like tribal flames.

'Yeah, we are,' Seb replies warmly.

I nod and smile at the stranger too.

'That's cool, man, so are we,' he comments, gesturing towards two other travellers who are walking back from the bar.

One of them is also muscular, but he's not quite as imposing as the American. He's not sporting any visible tattoos and his hair is long and blond, pulled up into a messy man bun. He's carrying a beer. A woman walks by his side. She's my age or a few years younger and she's holding a cocktail, her long silky ponytail swishing as she walks. She looks tanned and sporty and I notice a couple of guys checking her out as she approaches the table. She's dressed in skimpy clothes, hot pants a strappy vest that shows off her well-toned body. She has a bit of a cheerleader vibe and I think to myself how the guys look a bit like jocks. I take another sip of beer and try to quash my judgemental thoughts.

'I'm Cody,' the America guys, extending his hand.

'Hi Cody, I'm Seb,' Seb says, reaching over and shaking Cody's extended hand.

'I'm Rachel,' I add. Cody's hand is warm and dry, his handshake firm.

Cody's friends sit down with him, looking curiously at me and Seb.

'These guys are doing Everest too,' Cody explains.

I wince a little at his phrasing. Do you "do" Everest?

'Yeah, we're heading to base camp tomorrow,' Seb says, before introducing himself to Cody's friends.

The woman is Helen and the guy is called Joe. They seem

friendly enough. We chat a bit about our travels and it turns out that Cody met Joe in Thailand and they partied together for a few weeks before meeting Helen at their hostel in Bangkok. Helen had just finished a yoga retreat in Koh Phangan and they realised they were all planning to go to Nepal so they decided to travel together. Cody's a personal trainer from New York and apparently Joe was working as a bartender in Philadelphia. Helen explains how she was a personal assistant back home in Canada before getting wanderlust and saving up for a trip around Asia.

'I'm from Canada too,' Seb remarks. 'Where abouts are you from?'

'Quebec,' Helen says, smiling enthusiastically, revealing perfect pearly white teeth.

'Same!' Seb comments.

'No way!' Helen replies, smiling even more widely.

'I'm from Montreal!' Seb says.

'Same!' Helen balks.

'No way!' Seb replies, and they both start laughing.

They chat away about life in Montreal, which schools they went to, bars they hung out at, restaurants they miss. Cody, Joe and I nod along for a bit, but the conversation isn't exactly relatable. They start talking about some 'awesome' bar called The Coldroom that neither Cody, Joe or I have any opinion on.

'Wow, they really miss Canada, don't they?' Cody jokes, taking a sip of his beer.

'Yeah, I guess they do!' I reply, feeling a little bit uneasy.

I glance over at Seb. His eyes as sparkling as he talks about home. He's smiling widely, genuinely. I know he's a friendly person and he has a knack for engaging people, and he could just be doing a great job of having a nice conversation with a new person, but I can't help worrying that he's starting to miss home too, just like I have been. They've moved on from how great The Coldroom bar is to talking about some incredible Lebanese café that they both apparently frequented all the time. Seb's eyes are bright as they discuss it. What if Seb's secretly pining for his life back home? What if we're reaching the end of the road?

'I'm going to get some more beer. Do you guys want some?' Joe asks.

I glance at my bottle. I'm just over halfway down.

'Yeah, that would be great, thanks,' I reply.

Everyone else agrees to another drink and Joe heads off to the bar.

Helen and Seb are still going on about life back home. They've moved on from restaurants to gyms, although it turns out Seb hasn't heard of the yoga studio Helen frequents. Their conversation peters out a bit now that Joe's off at the bar and they turn to me and Cody.

'So, how did you two meet?' Cody asks, gesturing between me and Seb.

I feel secretly thankful to him for bringing me back into the conversation. Seb and I explain how we met at an ashram, which Cody and Helen both find fascinating. Particularly Helen.

'Which ashram?' she asks.

'The Hridaya ashram,' I tell her.

'You were staying at the Hridaya ashram? Oh my God!' she gushes, eyes wide.

'Yep!' I reply.

'I hear Guru Hridaya's an incredibly spiritual person,' Helen says dreamily. 'A true visionary.'

Seb and I exchange a look, unsure whether to go into what Guru Hridaya's really like with his dodgy track record of tax evasion, let alone my legal battle with him and my ban from even entering the ashram.

'Yes, his followers do say that,' I reply, not really wanting to go there.

'Definitely,' Seb agrees, smiling.

'Wow, what an amazing place to meet!' Helen enthuses.

'It was pretty magical!' I say, cringing at how cheesy I sound, even though I mean it. It was magical.

Helen asks about the ashram, from its infamous ornate pink temple to its highly-regarded yoga courses. Joe comes back with the beers, placing a tray down in the middle of the table. We all thank him.

Helen reaches for a fresh beer.

'So where are you from Rachel?' she asks. 'I got so distracted with Seb being from Montreal that I forgot to ask.'

So distracted by Seb in general, I think, before feeling guilty for being so bitter.

'I'm from London,' I tell her.

'London,' Helen echoes, sneering a little, as though "London" is a dirty word.

'Yes, London!' I laugh, feeling a little uncomfortable.

'I did an internship in London a few years ago. It would not stop raining. It was so expensive and oh my god, it was so busy too. Everyone's always in such a hurry there. They're always charging about, avoiding each other's gaze, marching to the office, jumping on the Tube!' she says.

I laugh awkwardly and take another swig of beer, feeling myself prickling with irritation. Helen clearly doesn't like London, but does she have to be so obvious about it? I mean, in a way, she's right. London is busy. It is stressful. The Tube is hot and dirty and over-crowded, and people do walk around with their heads down, looking miserable half the time. And it is expensive. But London isn't all bad. It's a fascinating place. There's always something interesting going on. So people aren't the friendliest and they do tend to be busy, but when you actually get chatting to Londoners, they're really warm and friendly. We don't all just head to the office being miserable. We do that, sure, but that's not all we do!

I start defending London, selling its cultural scene, its vibrant communities, its rich history, but I can tell Helen isn't really interested. She's swigging her beer and barely bothers to respond to my points.

'I haven't been to London, but I want to go. It sounds really cool,' Joe comments, smiling kindly.

I smile back. 'Yeah, it is cool.'

There's a lull in the conversation. Seb takes a swig of his beer.

'So where did you intern?' he asks Helen.

'Oh, at my dad's firm,' Helen replies. 'At his London office. In international relations.'

International relations?! I have to stop myself from rolling my eyes. Not only are these two both from Montreal but Seb did a degree in international relations.

He mentions it to Helen.

'Oh wow. Yeah, my dad has an international relations consultancy firm, Insights International. Their headquarters is in Montreal, but they have offices in a few in Europe and the US,' Helen replies casually, as though it's totally normal to have a dad who's an international business mogul.

'No way!' Seb utters, looking totally floored. 'I interned at Insights International.'

'What?! Seriously?' Helen gawps.

'Yeah!' Seb replies, and then they're off again, discussing the company, Helen's dad, Seb's internship, Helens work-life. Helen is more than just a little impressed when Seb tells her about his degree from the Sorbonne in Paris and I can't help noticing that the looks she gives him become more and more intense and flirtatious. Neither of them seems to be able to get over the coincidence that Seb interned at her dad's company.

Joe, Cody and I smile and look on, even though we're not even remotely involved in the conversation.

'What a small world!' Helen declares eventually.

'Definitely!' Seb agrees, shaking his head in disbelief. 'Crazy!'

Helen asks Seb what he's been up to since his internship and he visibly stiffens. He has a massive chip on his shoulder about his career. Even though Seb is really smart and has a great degree, he hasn't exactly put it to much use. He did a few internships and worked in international relations for a year or so after graduating, but he rapidly grew restless and unsatisfied with office life. He quit his job and got hired as a ski instructor at a plush resort where he drank too much with tourists and lived it up. His life actually got so hedonistic that he ended up crashing and burning and feeling like he had to escape. That's how he ended up in India, taking some time out. He felt the need to reconnect with himself and what really matters in life, beyond crazy nights out, sex and casual relationships. He's really turned over a new leaf here in India. He's read so many books on spirituality, from mainstream books like The Secret to more obscure texts like The Tibetan Book of the Dead and he's even been taking online courses in cognitive behavioural therapy and mindfulness. And his translation work has been going well too, but I know he still feels insecure about his career path. I think it stems from having been such an over-achiever at school; he feels he ought to be a high-flyer now but instead, things have taken a bit longer to come together for him. He's expressed his sense of shame over it in private conversations with me a few times, but I've tried to reassure him that he's doing fine and it will be okay. I know that when Seb figures out what he wants to do, he'll make it work. He's smart enough and diligent enough.

I've tried to remind him that there's so much more to life than your career too. Before I came to India, I was obsessed with my career to the point that I'd stopped noticing or caring whether or not I was having any fun in life. It took coming to the ashram for me to slow down a bit and realise there was more to life size than the size of my paycheck or my job title on LinkedIn. Seb thinks his career track record is something to be embarrassed about, but I wish he didn't feel that way. His appreciation of the truly important things in life, like being kind to people, enjoying nature, and even meditation, have made me become a better, happier person. He's so inspiring in a truly authentic way that has nothing to do with some job title.

While Seb and Helen chat about work, Joe and Cody are talking about Nepalese beer and comparing Nepali brands to the brands they have back home, carefully considering alcohol content, taste, even packaging. They're getting really into it and they both clearly loved their beer. I don't fit into either conversation.

'This is fab!' I comment, taking a sip of my beer.

They agree with me, but start talking about another beer brand I've never even heard of.

I shrink back into myself and take another sip. The beer feels like my only friend right now. And it is quite nice.

'My dad might have some job opportunities going,' I catch Helen saying to Seb.

I feel a pang of horror. Job opportunities? In Montreal?! We haven't even discussed our relationship. What's Seb going to do? Return to Montreal to take a job at Helen's dad's company? Oh God.

'Really?' Seb remarks, sounding keen.

'Definitely!' Helen replies, taking a swig of her beer, before rattling the bottle, realising it's empty.

'Fancy another drink?' she says to just Seb.

My beer is pretty much empty too, but she doesn't even look my way. She gets up.

'Come to the bar with me, I'll tell you about it,' she says to Seb.

'Okay.' Seb shrugs, seeming completely oblivious to how much Helen clearly fancies him.

I glance at his beer and see that he's barely had any. He's not a big drinker these days.

He turns to me.

'Are you coming?' he asks.

'No, I'm fine,' I reply, shrugging.

He narrows his eyes, as though not quite believing me.

'Really, I'm fine,' I insist.

Okay, so I might not feel fine exactly, but I can't exactly admit that I'm worried Seb's going to run off into the sunset with Helen from Montreal without looking like a total bunny boiler, can I?

'Cool, I'll be back in a minute,' Seb says, giving my shoulder a squeeze.

'Okay,' I reply with a smile.

Cody and Joe have moved on from talking about beer brands to discussing their fitness targets for Everest.

'I'm pretty sure I can do thirty kilometres a day,' Cody insists.

'Thirty-five, easy,' Joe retorts.

I try to act interested but I look off into the distance towards Helen and Seb at the bar. Helen is laughing at something Seb has said, throwing her head back dramatically. What is she laughing at? They're meant to be talking about job opportunities. How is that so hilarious? I take another swig of my beer.

'Do you mind if we smoke?' Cody asks, pulling a joint from his pocket.

'Oh, errr...' I hesitate, a little taken aback.

Surprisingly, no one I've met on my trip so far has been into drugs. People hardly drank alcohol in the ashram, let alone smoked pot or did anything harder. Even outside the ashram, I've never smoked pot, not once. I never had an interest in it as a teenager or at university. And I wouldn't touch it now. Maybe it's the lawyer in me but I'm just too straight-edge for that.

I think Joe must sense my unease.

'Dude smoke over there,' Joe says pointing across the bar towards a deserted area.

He shoots Cody a look.

'Okay.' Cody shrugs. 'You don't mind being on your own for a minute, do you, Rachel?'

'Not at all. Go for it,' I reply, smiling encouragingly.

'Alright, cool,' Cody says and they get up and go off to smoke their joint over by the balcony.

I'm not particularly bothered about being left alone. It kind of beats having to listen to them show off about Everest. And it beats pretending to be interested in a dissection of Nepalese versus US beer.

I take my phone out of my bag and check the WiFi is working. I have a couple of messages from Priya asking how things are going. I message her back telling her everything is great. I leave out Helen, Cody and Joe. After all, they're just some random travellers who will probably be out of our lives as quickly as they came. I message my Mum too giving her a quick update, even though I already messaged when we arrived last night to let her know our flight arrived safely. I scroll through Facebook for a minute and take another sip of my beer. My head feels weirdly hot and I have the urge to hold my cool bottle of beer against it, but I resist.

My hand feels sweaty, weirdly sweaty. Not just sweaty because I'm in Nepal and it's hot. It's a different kind of sweatiness. I touch my forehead and realise that it's beading with sweat too. My stomach starts churning. I assume it's hunger, but then it makes a strange gurgling noise that's so loud that I instantly glance over at the people sitting at the table next to me, half expecting them to have heard, but fortunately they seem completely oblivious. My stomach keeps churning, making weird noises. I think of that gross chicken from last night. I really shouldn't have eaten it. It was clearly dodgy. I mean, who in their right mind buys emaciated-looking chicken from a random roadside cart at 2am? My stomach makes even more strange noises.

Seb and Helen return from the bar, walking back to the table.

'Are you okay?' Seb asks, frowning, as he approaches.

'Yeah, I'm fine!' I reply brightly, plastering a smile onto my face.

'Where are Cody and Joe?' Seb asks as he sits down, handing me a beer.

I take the beer gratefully and point across the bar.

'They're just having a joint over there,' I say, pointing in their direction.

I find myself hoping Helen smokes pot and is about to go off and join them, but she doesn't. That would give me an opportunity to tell Seb what's happened. I need to get back to our room and sort myself out. Seb smiles at me and takes a sip of his beer, completely oblivious.

'I can't get over Seb knowing my dad!' Helen comments, smiling and shaking her head in disbelief.

'I know, what a coincidence!' I reply. 'Crazy!'

'Totally. All the way out here in Kathmandu and I meet someone who's interned at my dad's company. It's like, fate!' Helen enthuses.

'Yeah…' I agree, feeling uneasy.

She's making out like it's destiny that she and Seb, my boyfriend, have met.

'What are the chances!' I add.

Seb starts waxing lyrical about Helen's Dad, explaining to me some of the projects he's worked on, from providing guidance on international trade relations to promoting human rights legislation in far-flung corners of the world. It's quite impressive. Okay, very impressive. It's clear that Helen's dad is a very accomplished man. But I can't help wondering from the pointed way Seb keeps praising Helen's dad, whether he might be trying to impress her with his knowledge of international relations. Does he want a job? He has been talking about getting his career back on track recently. What if he sees running into Helen as a sign and decides to return to Montreal for a job at her dad's company? I'd love for Seb to find a job he's passionate about, but the idea of losing him is so hard.

'Hey guys,' Cody says.

He and Joe sit down, looking bleary-eyed and dopey. They're both moving a bit slower than they were before. The sun is setting and the bar is getting busier with more travellers having drinks and admiring the view over Kathmandu. A few groups are posing for pictures. The music gets turned up and the atmosphere starts to feel more like a club.

'Shall we dance?' Helen suggests, grinning excitedly.

A couple of other travellers have congregated in a dance floor area and are dancing, smiling and laughing and having a good time.

'Yeah, why not!' Joe says.

Cody shrugs, and gets up.

'Do you want to?' Seb asks me.

'No, I'm okay,' I reply, my stomach churning.

'Come on, Seb!' Helen says.

'Come on Rachel!' she adds, almost as an afterthought.

'It'll be fun!' Seb suggests to me.

'Yeah, it'll be fun!' Helen insists brightly.

'No, I'm cool. I'm just going to sit here and, erm, relax,' I insist. 'Take in the view.'

'Come on then, Seb!' Helen says, grabbing Seb's arm.

If I was in any doubt as to whether Helen fancied Seb, I'm not anymore. She's being so blatant about it.

'Are you sure you don't want to?' Seb asks me.

'No, I'm fine,' I reply.

Helen tugs Seb towards the dance floor. He rolls his eyes as she drags him away. They all start dancing among the throng of other travellers.

Great. I'm sitting here alone with a churning stomach, watching my boyfriend dance with a hot woman whose shiny ponytail seems to swish in time with the music. Brilliant. Just brilliant. Cody and Joe are terrible dancers, throwing themselves around the dancefloor, cutting shapes, completely out of time with the music. Helen dances like a stripper, her eyes fixed on Seb's. Could she be any more brazen? She turns around and starts twerking, while throwing her hair around. Mercifully, Seb looks awkward and backs away, dancing with Joe instead and Helen gives up on the twerking.

Another group of travellers join the dancefloor, obscuring my group from sight. My stomach lurches once more and I feel an overwhelming urge to go to the toilet. I really need to get back to the hotel room. The pressure builds inside me. I need to go *quick*.

Without giving it too much more thought, I grab my bag and get up and go. I hurry across the bar. I keep my eyes fixed on the exit. I make it and rush through the exit doors and into the hallway. I get into the lift and let out a sigh of relief as its doors close and it descends down the shaft towards my floor. My stomach is still churning, lurching uncomfortably as I let myself into mine and Seb's room. I rush to the ensuite bathroom and inspect my reflection. I'm pale and sweaty-looking. My pupils have become dilated. My stomach lurches again and I sit down on the toilet, my bowels unleashing. I find myself distantly musing over the irony that now that I've left India, I've finally got Delhi belly. That roadside chicken was definitely not a good idea.

My stomach twists and squirms and every time I think there can't possibly be anything left inside me, a new wave of diarrhea arrives. Just as I'm starting to wonder whether you can die from Delhi belly, it finally stops. Tentatively, I get up. I look at my reflection. I look awful. I'm white as a sheet and covered in sweat, my pupils are black saucers and my hair has gone frizzy. I splash some water onto my face and stagger into the bedroom where I grab a bottle of water and down the whole thing before collapsing onto my bed. I feel woozy and not quite with it. I think of Seb, at the bar, dancing with Helen and feel a wave of dread. I reach for my bag and find my phone. I want to message him and explain what's happened, but before I know it, I'm passing out, my phone falling from my hand onto the hotel room floor.

7 CHAPTER SEVEN

I open my eyes and see an overhead fan whirring above me. Sunlight fills the room and for a moment, I don't have a clue where I am and feel a wave of panic.

'Rachel?' Seb says.

I look over and see Seb lying next to me, his brow knotted with concern, and then it all comes flooding back: I'm in a hotel room in Kathmandu. And I've got Delhi belly, or Kathmandu belly, even though that doesn't have quite as good a ring to it.

'Are you okay?' Seb asks.

'What time is it?' I grumble.

Seb looks at his watch. 'Nine-thirty.'

I think of last night, Helen twerking against him.

'What happened last night?' I ask.

'What do you mean? We were dancing and then I looked over and saw you were gone so I went looking for you. I came to the room and found you passed out on the bed. Are you okay?' Seb asks, eyeing me with genuine concern. I still don't feel great. I feel woozy and weak.

'That chicken…' I utter.

Seb grimaces. 'Yeah, we should never have eaten that.'

He reaches for a glass of water on the bedside table and hands it to me with a few pills.

'Take these,' he says. 'Cody gave them to me. They'll help.'

'Cody?' I echo.

'Yeah,' Seb replies.

'Did you tell him?' I ask.

'Yeah, we were looking for you last night and then I found you up here. I told them you were unwell, and he just gave me some pills for food poisoning and headaches and stuff,' Seb explains.

'Oh, right.'

I take the pills and knock them back with a few gulps of water. My stomach lurches again. I groan, placing my hand on it.

'How are you doing?' Seb asks.

'Not great,' I admit.

'Do you want something to eat? Some bread? Would that help?' Seb asks. 'I can go and get you some.'

'No, I'm okay,' I reply, not quite ready to eat.

'Okay, are you sure?' Seb asks, looking anxious and fretful.

'Yeah, maybe later,' I suggest.

'Okay,' Seb replies.

I realise he has shadows under his eyes. He yawns.

'When did you wake up?' I ask.

'I don't know,' Seb says. 'I've just been snoozing on and off. I didn't want to properly sleep until I knew you were okay.'

As I wake up a bit more, I realise he's pulled his bed across the room so it's next to mine. He must have been watching me closely most of the night.

'Aww!' I reach out and stroke his arm. 'I just had diarrhea Seb, I wasn't dying!'

Seb smiles. 'Best to be on the safe side.'

I laugh. I want to lean over and kiss him, but my stomach is still cramping, and I don't feel up to moving. Plus, I'm probably not particularly kissable right now. Thinking of kissing, I suddenly think of Helen, who clearly wouldn't have minded locking lips with Seb.

'That girl from last night, Helen, was really into you!' I point out.

'What? Helen? No, she wasn't!' Seb scoffs.

'Umm yeah, she was! She was throwing herself at you, right in front of me,' I remind him. 'She was twerking!'

'Oh yeah, the twerking was a bit out there, but she was just messing around,' Seb says bashfully. 'We were all doing crazy drunk dancing.'

'Hmmm...' I murmur. 'She wasn't twerking against Cody and Joe. She was just twerking against you.'

'Nah!' Seb retorts.

'She was into you, it was so obvious.'

'She was just friendly,' Seb insists. 'It's such a weird coincidence that I knew her dad.'

'Yeah, it was weird, but she clearly likes you Seb, trust me,' I insist.

'She's Canadian. We're friendlier, that's all,' Seb protests.

He looks genuinely convinced that Helen's not interested.

'Very friendly!' I comment, giving him a pointed look.

'Don't worry about Helen, worry about getting better,' Seb comments. 'Are you sure you don't want some bread?'

I smile, warming to the idea.

'Okay, why not?'

'Cool.'

Seb gets to his feet. He's wearing jogging bottoms and a T-shirt and slips his feet into flip-flops.

'I'll be back in a minute. Are you going to be okay?' he asks.

'Yeah, I'll be fine.'

Seb smiles sweetly, even though he looks pale and exhausted. It's so adorable that he's stayed up all night, looking out for me. I feel a huge wave of love and affection for him.

'Seb?' I say, as he turns to leave.

'Yeah,' he replies.

'I...'

I want to ask him what's next for us. What's in store. Where are we heading after Everest? But the question is too big, to life-changing, and I don't know where to start. I don't know if I can cope with hearing the answer unless it's the one I want to hear.

'What is it?' Seb asks, looking concerned.

'Oh nothing,' I reply, batting the thought away. 'Don't worry about it.'

'Okay!' Seb laughs.

He heads out of the room, closing the door gently behind him.

I finish the glass of water Seb gave me and then get up and hobble to the bathroom. I look dreadful, deathly pale and clammy. Definitely not attractive. I sit down on the toilet and a new wave of diarrhoea pours out of me. Lovely, just lovely. Something's moving in the corner of my eyeline. I glance up to see a massive cockroach crawling over the wall. I shriek, and I'm about to jump up off the loo, before remembering that I'm midway through a diarrhoea explosion. Groaning, eyes fixed on the cockroach, skin crawling, I finish up on the toilet. I wash my hands and dash out of the bathroom, closing the door behind me with a shudder, aware of the cockroach still inside.

I think of my house back in London, my lovely plush colour-coordinated bathroom. I want to go home so badly. I'm done with travelling. I'm done with being overseas. I'm done with strange food and annoying people and disgusting insects. I sink back onto my bed. It creaks under me, feeling flimsy. I'm done with sleeping in uncomfortable beds in places that aren't quite where I belong. I miss my bed. I miss my friends. I miss food that doesn't make me ill. And yet I love Seb. I feel so torn. My stomach cramps again. I sigh.

I reach for my phone and text Priya.

Me: Haven't even set foot on Everest and I'm already feeling broken! Xx

I hit send.

FLYING DUO

8 CHAPTER EIGHT

'Hey Dad!' Seb says, waving at dad on his iPad.

'Hey son, how's it going?' His dad says.

I glance at the screen. I'm out of shot but I see his dad making dinner. He must have the iPad propped up on a windowsill or something. Seb and his dad look so alike. They're both tall and they share the same blue eyes, the same gap between their two front teeth, the same tanned skin. Seeing Greg, Seb's dad, is like looking into the future of what Seb might look like if we stay together long-term. However, even though they look alike, Seb and his dad are worlds apart when it comes to personality. Seb is sweet-natured and sensitive. He's spiritual and open-minded and loves to read. Whereas his dad is tough and competitive. He works as a construction manager and he has absolutely no interest in spirituality or books. He doesn't particularly approve of Seb's trip to India and the spiritual quest he embarked upon and believes meditation is 'for girls'. He kind of annoys me, but he's Seb's dad and despite his flaws, Seb loves him. He has travelled a bit though. He climbed Everest when he was twenty-five and I think, in a way, Seb is keen to follow in his footsteps.

'We're good, we're in Kathmandu,' Seb explains. 'The WiFi's a bit patchy but hopefully it will be alright.'

'Hi Greg!' I say, waving at the screen and plastering on a

smile.

I've spent the whole day in bed, nibbling on bread and trying to recover from my food poisoning. I'm starting to feel a lot better but I'm still tired and missing my home comforts.

'Hi Rachel, how are you doing?' Greg asks.

'I'm alright, thanks. Ate some chicken that didn't agree with me but I'm beginning to feel a bit better.'

'Ah sorry to hear that,' Greg says.

His pan sizzles. He flips a steak.

'Are you okay though?'

I nod. 'Yeah, I'll be fine,' I reply.

'That's good,' Greg says with a smile.

'How are you?' I ask him.

'I'm keeping well. Been out fishing today. Beautiful day,' Greg replies, moving his steak around in the pan. 'So when are you getting up the mountain then?'

'Whenever Rachel feels better,' Seb says.

Greg nods.

'So are you feeling prepared?' Greg asks as he tends to a pan of boiling potatoes.

Seb glances at me and shrugs.

'I think so, illness aside. We've got everything, from leech repellent to a compass.'

'Good. You'll definitely need it. And have you got your tent?' Greg asks.

'No Dad, we're just doing the base camp trek so we're staying in guesthouses,' Seb reminds him.

'Oh yes, I forgot you're not going all the way up,' Greg comments, with a sly smile.

I just about resist the urge to roll my eyes. Greg is well aware that we're not trekking to the summit of Everest, but it's like he'll find any excuse to remind Seb that our trek is inferior to his feat back in the seventies. He has a tendency to put Seb down a bit and I'm not sure if Seb doesn't see it or just doesn't want to. His dad is pretty much all the family he's got. His mum died of breast cancer when he was a teenager and ever since, his dad's been single. I think Seb cuts his dad a lot of slack because for years he was broken by grief.

'If we were climbing to the summit, we'd have had to be training for weeks, months,' Seb points out, sounding a bit exasperated.

'That's true. You didn't want to train, did you?' Greg says as he plates up his steak and potatoes.

'No, we didn't,' Seb states, quite assertively.

Seb rarely gets annoyed with his Dad, but I can tell that he's beginning to lose his patience. Greg must pick up on it too as his expression softens.

'Look, I'm sure you're going to have a great time. It'll be beautiful. Take lots of pictures,' he says.

'We will,' Seb replies, his voice still tense.

'So, when am I going to meet you Rachel?' Greg asks, changing the subject.

'Umm…' I utter, suddenly awkward.

Is he going to meet me? I have no idea. Seb and I have never mentioned visiting Montreal together.

'I mean, what's the plan? Will you be coming back to Montreal, Seb?' Greg asks.

My heart lurches. He went there. He actually went there. I glance at Seb, who looks as taken aback as I feel.

'Dad!' Seb tuts. He rolls his eyes. 'If we're coming to Montreal, we'll let you know, okay?'

'Okay!' Greg replies. He grins mischievously and spears a piece of steak onto his fork. He pops it into his mouth.

'Anyway, we'd better go. Have to get an early night before Everest!' Seb says.

'Alright!' Greg replies through a mouthful of steak. 'Well enjoy yourselves. Break a leg! Oh wait, actually don't.'

He starts laughing at his own joke. We laugh along

begrudgingly.

'See you!' Seb says.

'Bye Seb, bye Rachel!' Greg replies, waving at the screen as Seb hangs up.

The screen goes black and Seb lets out a sigh of relief, tossing his iPad down on the duvet next to him.

'God, he's such hard work!' I comment.

'That's just my dad for you!' Seb sighs.

I want to point out that his Dad is actually quite mean to him and maybe it's not okay, but I'm not sure whether I should. Seb looks up to his dad despite how difficult he can be.

A silence passes between us. I notice that Seb's frowning. I wonder if he's thinking about the question his dad asked about me and him, and when we're going to be in Montreal. The future of our relationship is beginning to feel like the elephant in the room. In a way, his dad is being braver than either of us by bringing it up. Someone has to. And yet the moment Greg mentioned our future, Seb immediately shut him down. Why? Does he not want to break it to me that this is just a holiday romance? A long, intense, extremely heartfelt holiday romance, but a holiday romance nonetheless?

'Seb...' I utter.

'Yeah,' Seb replies, looking over at me with a curious expression.

I'm going to bring it up, ask him what the future holds for us, but suddenly, I lose my nerve.

'Shall we get dinner at that momo place down the road?' I suggest instead, losing my nerve.

We passed a momo restaurant on the way back to the hotel yesterday that looked amazing.

'Are you feeling up to it?' Seb asks.

'Yeah, I'm feeling fine,' I reply.

'Perfect,' Seb says. 'Sounds good.'

9 CHAPTER NINE

'Are you sure you're okay?' Seb asks, for what feels like the twenty-seventh time as we make our way to the bus stop to catch the bus to Kathmandu.

'Yeah, I'm fine!' I laugh.

I genuinely feel fine now. It's been a few days since I was unwell, and it's now passed completely. It's a bright day, the sky is azure blue, and the sun is glowing. I'm finally beginning to feel positive about climbing Everest. Okay so it's not my dream holiday activity, but I'm going to make the most of it.

'Okay, cool,' Seb replies, smiling, the sun beaming down on him, making his blue eyes shimmer. 'This is going to be great. Imagine if the weather is like this while we're up in the mountains. The views are going to be-'

'Seb!' A voice interrupts Seb's musings.

We turn around and see Cody and Joe, with Helen trailing behind them. They're kitted out like us, with backpacks on, hiking boots tied by their laces to the straps. Oh no. They're heading to Everest too.

'You guys heading to base camp?' Joe asks.

'Yeah! We're on our way to get the bus,' Seb explains.

'Cool! So are we!' Joe enthuses.

'Are you feeling better, Rachel?' Cody asks, looking genuinely concerned.

'Yeah, thanks. I'm fine,' I reply, feeling a little self-conscious.

'That's great!' Cody grins. 'We were worried about you. I got ill when I first arrived in Thailand. Couldn't remove myself from the toilet for three days straight,' he says.

'Eww!' Helen replies.

I laugh awkwardly, feeling a little self-conscious.

As we make our way to the bus stop, Cody regales us all with a detailed account of his food poisoning experience, which was apparently brought on by eating deep fried crickets from a market stall in Bangkok, as we lumber towards the bus stop. The guys are stronger than me and Helen and we both drop behind slightly.

She looks at me and gives me a friendly smile. I smile back, trying to think of something to say.

'So, are you looking forward to this then?' I ask, thinking that we might be able to establish some female camaraderie over this gruelling Everest trek.

'Absolutely, it's going to be amazing. I can't wait!' Helen enthuses. 'I absolutely love hiking! I go all the time back home.'

'Oh wow, great!' I reply, not even remotely able to relate. The closest I've come to hiking in recent years is walking up the hill in Greenwich Park.

'There's nothing quite like doing a hike, you know? Connecting with nature, the fresh air, the physicality of it. You know?'

'Oh definitely! It's the best,' I reply, smiling brightly.

'There's our bus!' Joe says, pointing after at a bus driving past us.

He picks up his pace and starts running after it. He's so strong and fit that running even with his backpack looks effortless. I try to quicken my pace, but I feel sweaty and breathless.

'Why are we running? Won't it stop?' I ask Seb, who is doing a sort of half-run, half-walk after Joe and the bus.

'Well, hopefully. But there are only two buses running a day so we don't want to miss it,' Seb says as he carries on hurrying after the bus.

Joe keeps running, waving his arm after the bus as though to flag it down. It draws to a halt at a stop in the distance and Joe slows down a bit, but then the bus starts moving again. It disappears from sight.

'What the hell? It's left!' he exclaims.

'Where's it going?' Cody shouts down the road towards him.

'It's gone. It stopped and then just drove off. I can't believe this,' Joe shouts back.

We head down the road until we reach the bus stop. It's deserted.

'There must have been one or two passengers to pick up and then the driver decided not to wait around,' Joe comments, shaking his head, looking aggrieved.

His disappointment is palpable.

'When's the next bus?' I ask.

'Not for six hours,' Joe sighs.

He slumps on a nearby wall and pants, catching his breath.

We all take a seat on the wall, resting. I look around. There's not much on the street, it's just a dull, boring road at the outskirts of the city. There aren't any nice cafés where we could go and kill time. I guess we'll have to head back to the city centre and find somewhere to wait there. Although, as I look further down the road, I spot a group of tourists getting onto another bus. It's not like the bus we were going to catch. Our bus was plush and modern and this bus looks rickety and old, but the people getting on it look like they might be hikers. They've got backpacks like us and a few of them are wearing hiking boots.

'Do you think that bus might be heading to Everest?' I ask the group, pointing into the distance.

'I don't know,' Joe replies, shrugging. He's panting slightly now, catching his breath.

'I reckon we should go and find out,' I suggest.

'Yeah, why not?' Cody replies.

We start walking towards the other bus. As we approach, I overhear the group chatting and realise they're Spanish. Fortunately, I studied Spanish at school and catch a few words of their conversation. They're discussing trekking and base camp. They're heading to Everest.

I turn to Seb, Cody, Joe and Helen and tell them enthusiastically.

Joe looks sceptical. 'We can't just get on their bus though,' he says.

'We could ask!' I reply, undeterred.

I approach the group. They filter onto the bus. I wait until they've all got on and have settled down into their seats. I spot a few free seats at the back, enough for us. I step onto the bus. The driver looks Spanish too and I find myself wondering if this is some private tour, a big group of friends travelling together. Maybe Joe was right and we should just stick to the tourist bus. The driver looks at me expectantly, clearly wondering what I want.

'Hi, err…'

'Puedo ayudarte?' the driver asks.

I do a quick mental translation. Can he help me? I clear my throat and concentrate, trying to string together a sentence in my rusty Spanish.

'¿Podemos coger este autobús?' I ask, feeling pretty proud of my language skills, having cobbled together the question of whether we can take the bus.

Yet, all of a sudden, the passengers start laughing. Giggling and tittering. The driver's face twists into an amused smirk and he bursts into laughter too.

What the hell? I just asked if we could take the bus to Everest? Why is that so funny? I laugh awkwardly, having no idea what the joke is.

I look over my shoulder at Joe and Cody and Helen to see if they're inexplicably amused to, but they look blank. The passengers on the bus are still sniggering. Do I have something on my face? What's going on?

All I said was whether we can take the bus.

Urghh. I'm about to turn around and get off, when a girl sitting on one of the front seats of the bus catches my eye. She looks around my age, Spanish, with long shiny dark hair.

'In Argentinian Spanish "cojet" means to "fuck",' she tells me.

Oh God. According to my GCSE Spanish, "cojet" means "to take". So instead of asking if I can take the bus, I asked if I could fuck it. Great. Just great.

'I see,' I reply.

No wonder they're all laughing. I'm the awkward Brit who politely asks if she can copulate with buses.

I look over my shoulder at Seb. Even he's sniggering now. Joe Cody and Helen are cracking up, in on the joke now too. I roll my eyes. I decide to tell the driver that I'm very embarrassed in the hope he can just let us on and we can move on from this joke that I'm a bus shagger.

'Yo soy muy embarazado,' I tell the him.

He starts laughing even harder.

'¿Has tenido sexo con muchos autobuses últimamente?' he says.

Huh? He spoke quickly, saying something along the lines of whether I've been having sex with a lot of buses.

'I didn't catch that,' I say in English. I look to the girl with the long hair.

'He asked if you've been having sex with lots of buses lately. "Embarazado" means pregnant,' she explains.

'I see!' I reply.

The driver is still sniggering. Seb, Cody, Joe and Helen are chuckling away too.

So much for my save-the-day mission to get us onto the bus. Instead, I've become a laughing stock.

'Okay very funny!' I comment, rolling my eyes indulgently,

before turning to get off the bus.

'Espere,' the driver says.

Wait?

I turn back to him.

'Vamos, puedes venir gratis,' the driver says.

I look at him, confused, not quite grasping what he's saying.

'He says you can come on for free,' the girl in the front row seat says.

I turn to her, shocked.

'Really?'

'Si,' she replies. 'Yes.'

'What about my friends?' I ask her. 'Can they come on too?'

She asks the driver.

The driver replies. He's smiling at me now, looking kinder and good-natured.

'Yes, he says you and your friends are very welcome,' she says.

'Oh wow! Thank you!' I enthuse.

'Gracias. Mucho gracias!' I say to the driver, feeling relieved and grateful. Maybe coming across as a bus shagger was worth it after all.

'De nada! De nada!' The driver says, beckoning me and the others on board.

I thank him again.

'De nada. Trata de no quedar embarazada,' he says.

'Huh?' I reply.

'He said "try not to get pregnant" the girl explains.'

I roll my eyes and laugh.

'I'll try!' I insist as I make my way on board.

10 CHAPTER TEN

The bus journey to Everest takes hours, but it's only once we get close that the jokes about me copulating with buses start to wane. Cody and Joe have found the entire thing hilarious, along with the other passengers, who have asked me a range of questions, from calling me and an old banger to asking whether I get tired from my relations with buses or if they send me into overdrive. I've laughed along and vowed to be a bit more careful when speaking Spanish in the future. Finally, the bus jokes are replaced by awe at the sight of Everest. It soars into the sky, vast and imposing, glacial and magnificent.

We all lean towards the windows, taking pictures with our cameras and phones. The sight is genuinely awe-inspiring. Maybe this will be an exciting adventure after all.

'Oh man, this is going to be amazing!' Cody enthuses.

'It's going to be incredible,' Joe says.

'Definitely,' Seb concurs, his eyes sparkling with excitement.

Helen peers calmly through her camera, taking pictures.

While I am starting to feel slightly more excited about the trek, I can't help wondering whether Seb and I are going to be able to shake off Helen, Joe and Cody. Seb and I were meant to be spending time together on this trip. I thought we'd have a chance to discuss our future and figure out what's next, but now it seems likely that we're going to be trekking as a group. Especially since it turns out that Cody, Joe and Helen not only aimed to get the same bus as us, but also booked the same guesthouse too.

Helen examines a shot on her camera. 'Wow... I can't believe we're here!' she enthuses.

'Once in a lifetime, man, once in a lifetime!' Cody remarks.

I'm beginning to realise that Cody adds "man" to pretty much every sentence it seems regardless of the gender of the person he's speaking to.

'I'm so psyched!' Joe says.

'Yeah, it's going to be great,' Helen comments.

'Can't wait!' I add as the bus crawls up higher up the mountain path.

The roads are narrow, and yet our driver is speeding along them fast and confidently, like he's on a motorway. You'd think he might adopt a bit of caution while driving along perilous mountain roads in a rickety old claptrap, but apparently not. I find myself clutching the sides of my seat, my palms sweating.

'I wish he's slow down,' I grumble to Seb.

'That's what she said,' Cody quips, still not quite ready to relinquish the lame bus-inspired sex jokes.

I roll my eyes, hoping I don't die on this bus. I don't want one of my last ever memories to be a joke that bad.

Seb reaches for my hand and gives it a squeeze. He smiles at me, excitement sparkling in his eyes and I smile back, squeezing his hand. I must feel Helen looking at me as I look her way to find her watching me and Seb with a sort of sad, wistful expression on her face. Realising I'm looking, she quicky looks away. I glance back at Seb, but he's gazing out of the window at Everest and clearly didn't notice Helen watching us. Helen's leaning towards the window again now with her camera, snapping away at Everest.

My hand grows increasingly sweaty in Seb's as the driver of our bus takes on hairpin bends like he's a Formula One racer. By the time we finally arrive at base camp, I'm a sweaty wreck. Even

Cody and Joe are looking a bit fraught and anxious. We get off the bus, thanking the driver in spite of his crazy driving.

'Did you have a good ride?' he asks me in English, winking.

The passengers nearby start sniggering.

'Ride of my life,' I joke.

He laughs.

Joe scrutinizes a map as we get off the bus.

'I think it's this way,' he says, pointing down a path leading off the main road.

We head down the path. The air feels clear and fresh up here and the scenery is incredible. Breath-taking. All around us are mountain peaks, jagged towering

'Here it is!' Joe says, pointing at a guesthouse with a handmade sign above a front door.

It's an unassuming-looking place and I find myself thinking what a funny coincidence it is that we would have ended up booking the exact same guest house as Cody, Joe and Helen. It's almost as though some twist of fate is bonding us with them for this trip. Seb believes in signs and messages from 'the universe' and all that sort of stuff. He's probably reasoning that there's some bigger purpose to us meeting them, whereas I just feel mildly irritated by it.

Joe knocks on the door and a Nepalese woman answers. She introduces herself as Hanka and welcomes us in with a big friendly smile. We filter into a large open-plan living room and kitchen. The guesthouse has a homely, lived-in feel and seems to be an extension of Hanka's home. We take off our backpacks and Hanka tells us to take a seat on the living room sofas, while she goes to make tea. She asks us where we're from.

We tell her.

'Ah, I see! So you met travelling? Or Helen and Seb, are you together?' she asks.

'No!' I pipe up, feeling a little unnerved. 'Seb and I are together. We met in India, actually.'

'Yes,' Seb replies.

Helen smirks.

'Seb and I just happen to be from the same place,' she explains to Hanka.

I smile awkwardly even though I'm feeling increasingly tense.

'I see,' Hanka says as she hands us cups of tea.

As I sip the tea, I start to feel a bit more relaxed. Hanka's house is lovely and homely, with an incredible view from the front room of the mountains, stretching into the distance, the sun setting behind them. Despite Cody and Joe being a bit competitive, they are very well-mannered and polite to Hanka, asking her questions about the area, her life growing up here. It turns out Joe has even done a crash course in Nepali and can speak to her in her native language, which Hanka seems to really appreciate.

'How do you feel about your trek?' she asks us. 'Excited?'

'Can't wait!' Helen enthuses.

'Yes, it should be great' I chime in. 'Although I'm a little nervous too.'

'Oh, don't worry,' Hanka replies, smiling warmly. 'It's mostly very safe.'

'Mostly?' I echo.

'Yes. These days it's very safe to trek across base camp. One three or four people die a year,' she tells us casually.

I look towards Seb, horrified. He said it was totally safe!

'Three or four?' I croak.

Hanka nods. 'Some fall. Some get really bad altitude sickness and some just disappear,' she tells us.

'Disappear?!' I echo, alarmed.

Is this going to be it? So much for the future of mine and Seb's relationship, what if we don't even make it out of this trek alive?

'Yes, the mountains are vast. Some tourists go trekking on their own. They think they know where they're going and then they just disappear. They're never seen again. It doesn't happen that much though,' Hanka says.

That much? Oh God.

'You should be okay because you're in a group. Most of the tourists that disappear are trekking alone,' Hanka explains.

I smile weakly. I thought this was going to be an easy trek!

Once we finish the tea, she shows us to our bedrooms. Cody and Joe are shown to a twin room, Helen has her own single room and then Seb and I are shown to our room.

Hanka opens the door.

'Here you go. Make yourself at home,' she says.

Like the hostel in Kathmandu, the room is sparse, with twin beds. It has dark stone walls and bears more than a passing resemblance to a cave. In fact, it makes our hotel room in Kathmandu seem quite cosy. But we thank Hanka and head inside, putting our bags down and closing the door behind us.

'Twin beds!' I whisper as Hanka's footsteps retreat down the corridor.

Seb laughs. 'I don't think we're going to be getting many king-sized doubles on this trip,' he comments, undoing the laces of his boots.

'No, it doesn't seem like it,' I sigh, feeling a little despondent.

So much for saving our relationship. This trip is turning into the least romantic experience ever.

I lie down the bed.

'Oh well,' I grumble.

'I don't think it's too bad though...' Seb ventures, his voice low and a bit sultry.

'Huh?'

I glance over and see him kicking off his shoes. He gets up and comes over to my bed, crawling on top of me.

'I don't think we need to let twin beds stop us from having fun,' he says.

I smile.

'No, we don't need a double bed to have fun,' I concur as I trace my hands over his back, relishing his warmth of his body and his familiar smell, both comforting and sexy.

'No, we don't,' Seb says, nuzzling my neck.

'Twin beds are quite underrated actually,' I reply melting under his touch as he kisses me.

11 CHAPTER ELEVEN

We wake up at 6am as the sun rises and the birds begin to chirp.

I blink, momentarily confused by the stone walls of the room I'm in, and then I remember where we are. I gaze up at the ceiling. I feel so well-rested, having had a deep and dreamless sleep. Maybe it's the fresh Himalayan air or something to do with the altitude. I make a mental note to Google that later. Seb is still fast asleep in his bed next to me, snoring gently, cocooned in his sleeping bag. He was right that bringing sleeping bags was a good idea. It got surprisingly cold last night and I was grateful we'd brought them with us since the guesthouse blankets are pretty thin. I sit up and open the window by my bed. A gentle breeze sweeps into the room. The air smells like it's been raining overnight. It's damp and yet so natural and pure. Beautifully clean.

I lie back down and listening to the chirping birds. Having had a good restorative night's sleep, I feel enthusiastic about the day ahead. So Cody, Joe and Helen might be a bit annoying, but I'm still in the Himalayas with the man I love. This is a once in a lifetime opportunity and I'm going to make the most of it. The scenery is stunning and I'm so lucky to be here. And even if I don't have the future all mapped out with Seb and it's bugging me a bit, I'm still going to treasure this experience with him at least.

Eventually the sound of the birds chirping wakes Seb up. We

shower and head downstairs for breakfast. Hanka is already in the kitchen.

'Good morning,' she says. 'How did you sleep?'

'So well!' I enthuse. 'Best night's sleep I've had in ages.'

Hanka smiles. 'Everyone says that. You will sleep very well on your trip.'

I smile. 'Hope so.'

She gestures towards the table where there's a bowl of bread, a plate of dosas and a pot of coffee. My stomach rumbles at the sight of it.

'Take a seat,' she says.

We thank Hanka and sit down. She places some sambar – a lentil stew - for the dosa and some butter for the bread, pours us glasses of juice and then leaves us to it. We thank her and she heads off to read a newspaper on the porch. I reach for a dosa. One of the things I've loved about Asia is the savoury breakfasts. I'll take dosa and sambar over cereal any day of the week.

'Helen and co must still be in bed,' I comment.

'Yeah, they must be,' Seb replies, taking a dosa from the plate too.

'You don't think we can make a run for it, do you?' I joke.

Seb smirks. 'Oh, come on, they're not that bad!'

'Well, Helen's a bit annoying,' I point out.

'She's fine!' Seb says.

One of the reasons I love Seb is because of his ability to see the good in people and get along with everyone. His effortless kindness and charisma were some of the first things that drew me to him. But even though I still love those qualities about him, they do have their downsides. Namely, that sometimes when he's seeing the best in people, he can be blinded to their negative qualities or behaviour.

'She's into you! Trust me,' I point out as I dip my dosa in sambar. 'She was looking at you weirdly on the bus ride.'

'Weirdly?' Seb echoes.

'Like, I don't know, kind of longingly,' I tell him.

'Well, I am irresistible,' Seb says with a totally straight face. 'You know that.'

'You're okay, I guess,' I tease, rolling my eyes.

Seb smiles. He reaches for the coffee and pours some into my cup.

'Well, I'm with you, aren't I? I'm your okay boyfriend,' he says.

'Suppose,' I sigh, tearing off a bite of dosa.

Seb frowns as he pours his own coffee before setting the pot down.

'You're not really worried about it, are you?' he asks.

'I'm not worried, it's just not overly romantic having her lingering in the background, lusting after you,' I comment, feeling a bit glum at the thought.

'I really don't think she's lusting, but even if we did want to get rid of them, how would we?' Seb asks. 'We can't just ditch them and go our own way. Everyone follows the same hiking route at base camp so we'll probably end up running into them. There are only a couple of guesthouses at each stop along the trek so it's pretty likely that we'll end up staying at the same places,' Seb muses. 'And anyway, I think they're alright. Cody's cool and Joe's great at map-reading. It might be good to have them trekking with us, and it's safer to trek in a group than it would be on our own.'

'I guess so,' I reply, realising he's right. We can't just ditch them. We're basically stuck with them now whether we like it or not.

'Morning!' Helen says, interrupting my thoughts.

She flounces into the room, ponytail swishing as usual, a big bright smile plastered over her face. She's wearing a miniscule pair of hot pants with a thin nearly see-through t-shirt over the top. I can't help noting that she does have an amazing body. She's so toned and yet has curves in all the right places. I find myself biting hard and somewhat angrily on my dosa as I note this fact.

'Morning,' Seb replies, smiling in his usual friendly way. 'How are you doing?'

'I'm fabulous! Slept like a log,' Helen gushes.

I see what Hanka means. Maybe everyone does sleep well here.

'So did we. Do you want coffee?' Seb asks.

'Ohhh coffee!' Helen replies, sitting down next to Seb. 'I'd love some.'

She smiles prettily at Seb and I feel a twinge of satisfaction as he doesn't notice and instead just pour the coffee into her cup.

'Are Joe and Cody up?' I ask.

'I think so,' Helen replies.

She thanks Seb for the coffee and brings it to her lips, inhaling its smell before taking a sip.

She smiles. 'God, I feel so well rested,' she says.

'I know. We slept really well too. Must be the air up here or something,' I comment.

'Yeah, and everything is just so dark,' Helen adds. 'No streetlights, no buildings, no traffic.'

'And it's so silent at night here too,' Seb adds.

'Totally,' Helen replies. 'Complete silence. It's so peaceful.'

We tuck into breakfast as Helen waxes lyrical about the sense of inner calm she feels up here. I get the feeling she's trying to impress Seb, knowing he's into that sort of thing, but I tell myself that maybe I'm just being paranoid. After all, she was doing a yoga retreat in Thailand before she met Cody and Joe so she is into spiritual stuff. And if we're going to be spending a few more days together, I should try to give her more of a chance. Hopefully she'll lose interest in Seb soon enough.

Cody and Joe appear, looking fresh from the shower, their hair still wet. They're already dressed in shorts and T-shirts and hiking boots, ready for the trek.

'Morning guys! How's it going?' Cody says as he and Joe sit down. 'Beautiful day.'

We chat about the day ahead as Hanka comes back and tops up

the coffee, pouring glasses of juice for everyone and replenishing the food on the table. We thank her and suggest she joins us, but she says she's already eaten and heads back onto the porch to read her paper. I have another dosa, feeling really hungry. The long night's sleep has given me an appetite, as well as last night's exertions with Seb. Although everyone seems to be tucking in. Cody packs away bread, eggs and two dosas. Even Helen polishes off three slices of toast.

'Got to fuel up for the trek!' Cody remarks, as he reaches for another slice of bread.

Finally, when we're done, we head back to our rooms and get ready. Seb and I pack our bags and I put on my hiking boots for the first time. They're enormous and make my legs feel like twigs.

'Are these really necessary?!' I ask Seb, raising an eyebrow as I kick a leg back, striking a pose.

'Yes, we're hiking Everest. Of all the occasions you could need hiking boots, this is it!' Seb laughs.

'I guess you're right,' I reply.

When we return downstairs, Cody and Joe are waiting, ready to go. They're huddled over a map in the kitchen. Joe looks over his shoulder and spots us.

'Hey guys. So how many kilometres do you reckon you can handle today? We're thinking 20?' he says.

'Twenty?' I echo, looking to Seb. Twenty kilometres is twelve miles.

Seb shrugs. 'Yeah, we can handle that,' he says.

I raise an eyebrow, hoping he's right.

Helen appears, wearing a tank top, combat trousers and hiking boots, with a compass dangling around her neck. She looks like a quintessential hiker, her backpack already strapped to her back.

'Ready?' she asks.

'Ready,' I reply, heaving my backpack onto my back.

'Cool!' Cody says, picking up the map.

We say goodbye to Hanka, settle our bill and leave the

guesthouse.

'Namaskar,' she says, meaning "goodbye" in Nepali.

'Namaskar,' we echo.

'Good luck,' she calls after us as we make our way from the guesthouse towards the Everest trail.

12 CHAPTER TWELVE

I know climbing Everest is meant to be a test of endurance, it's not exactly meant to be easy, but while everyone talks about the incredible sights and the physical and mental challenge of climbing the world's biggest mountain, no one talks about the other, more minor challenges you encounter when trekking in the Himalayas.

Such as the leeches. Seb may have bought leech repellent but I didn't realise quite how many leeches I'd have to contend with. Blood-sucking leeches. They keep latching themselves to my ankles as I walk. Apparently, they come out after it's been raining. Cody read about them online. You don't notice them at first, since when they attach themselves to you, it's pretty much painless. You only notice when you start to feel a stinging sensation and then you look down and see a little dark worm-like thing dangling off your skin, growing fat from your blood. It's like something from a horror film and it makes me queasy every time. Although they seem to like me for some reason. I must have tasty blood.

Cody spotted the first one, which was feasting on my calf, his eyes lighting up.

'Dude you've got a passenger!' he said, pointing at my leg.

Naturally, I shrieked and started freaking out.

'Seb!' I yelped. 'Give me the leech repellent?!'

Seb eyed the leech on my leg in horror and began rooting

around in his backpack for the leech repellent.

'Leech repellent?!' Cody echoed. 'That stuff's not going to work! Calm down. I know exactly what to do! Stay still.'

He then 'twisted off' the leech, grabbing it between his fingers and twirling it off my skin while I winced. It stung but it wasn't unbearable. Although blood started pouring from the spot where the leech had been feasting.

'What they do is inject an anti-coagulant that stops your blood clotting, so you just keep bleeding,' Cody said, sounding fascinating as he gazed in wonder at my dripping wound.

'I'll keep bleeding?' I gawped, looking desperately at Seb. He didn't warn me about this!

I began to feel a bit queasy as the blood dripped into my sock.

'There's a plant that helps the blood clot,' Cody said. 'It's called a Melastoma. I read about it. It's got long thin leaves and a red stalk.'

He went rooting around in the shrubbery, trying to find it.

When he did, he tore off a handful of leaves and stuffed them into his mouth.

'What are you doing?!' I asked, completely shocked.

We all looked at him like he was mad.

'You have to chew it into a pulp,' he explained, before spitting the chewed-up leaves out onto his palm. 'And then you stick it onto the wound.'

He crouched down next to me and stuck a globule of leaf pulp onto my wound.

'Eww!' I exclaimed, feeling the warm wet pulp on my skin.

'It'll help the blood coagulate,' he insisted.

'How do you know all this stuff?' Seb asked, impressed.

'I've been wanting to go to Everest since I was a teenager,' Cody said. 'I've been researching it for years.'

It may have felt a bit weird to have a globule of leaf pulp on my leg, but it did seem to stop the blood from trickling down into my sock. That is, until the next leech got me.

The other thing I had no idea about were the donkeys.

Don't get me wrong, I like donkeys. They're adorable. But there are so many of them. I didn't really realise how many local people there use the paths along the base camp trail just to get from A to B. They transport goods between the different villages on the back of donkeys, which they lead along the mountain paths. It makes you feel like you've gone back in time to another century. It's actually quite adorable seeing the donkeys hobbling past, but what's not so cute is having an American by your side who has taken to shouting "yak attack" every time they come by. It was funny-ish the first, maybe even second time, but Cody must have said it a dozen times now and I'm beginning to wonder if I could get away with pushing him off a steep ledge.

And there are the flimsy bridges. Walking along a mountainside is scary enough, but crossing narrow, fairly insubstantial bridges suspended between mountains with perilous drops beneath is not fun. We've already crossed five or six today and it's only day one. I hope they peter out soon as they're pretty intense. Another thing no one seems to mention is the sporadic toilets. It's okay for the guys. I think they find pissing into the shrubbery part of the rugged Everest experience, but I'm not exactly as keen. The last thing I need is nettles tickling my nether regions. Or worse, a leech attaching itself to my lady parts. And then there are the blisters. It's only day one and I've already had to put three plasters on my heels, despite my hiking boots. I dread to think what my feet are going to look like by the time we reach the end of the trek. Even though I have a massive plaster stuck on my heel, it still rubs every time I take a step.

'Oh wow!' Joe enthuses, heaving his bag off his shoulder and onto a rock. 'Now that is a photo moment!' He gazes at the sun setting between two snow-capped mountains.

The sun burns orange between them and glints prettily off their snowy peaks, making them appear golden. It's a gorgeous sight, heavenly almost.

Joe takes his digital SLR from around his neck and begins
trying to frame the photo perfectly, testing different angles,
crouching down and standing up. Joe, apparently, is a bit of a
photography pro. He told us earlier that he studied Photography
and Media Studies at university. Apparently, he does a bit of
freelance work, mostly portrait photography, but supplements his
income by working at a bar. He's shown us a few of the pictures
he's taken on the trek so far and they have been brilliant –
perfectly composed, sharply defined, the lighting on point. They
definitely beat the sort of amateur snapshots Seb and I tend to take,
which often feature a thumb.

Joe takes a few shots and then reviews them, scrolling through
them and examining the reel on the back of his camera.

Helen peers over his shoulder.

'Stunning!' she exclaims.

'The lighting's not quite right,' Joe replies.

He carries on taking pictures.

'Could you take a picture of me, Seb?' Helen asks, turning to
Seb, holding out her digital camera.

'Sure,' Seb says, taking the camera from her.

'Fab, thanks!' Helen replies.

She turns around to inspect the rocks behind her. One of them
is a prayer rock. They're dotted alone the Everest path—huge
rocks with prayers painted over them in Nepali. They're meant to
be good omens for hikers. Helen clambers onto a big one and
stands on it, looking epic against the setting sun. A breeze blows
through her hair and she strikes a pose, looking like some kind of
Greek goddess on a plinth.

'That's not extra, at all,' Cody jokes.

I snigger. Even Seb starts laughing.

'When I'm looking back on this photo and I'm old and grey,
I'll be grateful for being extra right now,' Helen remarks, pouting.

Seb peers through the lens. He moves a little to the right, trying
to frame Helen so the sun is shining behind her. He seems to be

taking a leaf from Joe's book.

Helen strikes a pose with one hand on her hip and looks off profoundly into the distance.

Joe looks her way and snorts.

I try to supress laughter but it's difficult.

'Seriously?' Joe jokes.

'Shut up Joe!' Helen hisses and resumes her pose.

Seb takes a few snaps.

'Take more,' Helen says. 'Like five or six, at least.'

Seb snaps away. As we've been walking, we've been chatting a bit more about our lives. It turns out that Helen is an Instagram influencer. Her handle is @hippyishhelen. I haven't seen her account myself yet since the WiFi signal isn't exactly great up Everest, but Helen showed us some of the pictures she posts: shots of her sipping from coconuts on beaches, lying in hammocks while sunbathing in skimpy bikinis and meditating in temples. It's all very wholesome and yet sexy and she captions most pictures with statements like 'yesterday is history, tomorrow is a mystery and today is a gift, that's why we call it the present' and 'it's not the number of breaths we take, but the number of moments that take our breath away', alongside the hashtags #blessed and #journey. Her quest to get the perfect snap means that whenever she has her picture taken, she likes whoever is taking it to take around twenty shots. Then she reviews them and then she has another twenty shots taken, and repeat, until she gets an Instagram-worthy shot. She found an 'instagrammable' tree earlier and posed next to it for about 120 pictures, taken by Joe, until she finally got a shot she liked. I don't think any of us factored all the photo sessions into our daily hikes.

Helen poses on the rock while Seb snaps away. Eventually, she hops down and inspects Seb's pictures.

'Oh my God!' she balks, her eyes widening at one of the shots he's taken. 'That is absolutely perfect!'

She eyes him with absolute awe, like he's Rankin. I love Seb and everything, but his photography credentials extend to snaps of butterflies perching on rocks and out-of-focus selfies.

Helen inspects the shot closely.

'Wow! This is perfect. I'm going to break the gram with this one,' she says.

'Break the gram?!' I echo.

Helen ignores me. I take a look at the picture. She's standing in a halo of golden light, the mountains stretching behind her. It is a good shot.

'Thanks, Seb!' she gushes. 'I cannot wait to post this!'

'No worries,' Seb replies sweetly.

I sigh, look further along the path, hoping we don't have too far to walk until we get back to our guesthouse. Unlike Helen, who is still glowing and instagrammable, I'm covered in leech bites. I feel knackered and hungry and I keep thinking about how much I could demolish a plate of momos.

'Rachel,' Joe says, interrupting my thoughts. 'Do you want me to take a picture of you and Seb?'

'Sure!' I reply, brightening instantly.

I take my camera from my neck and pass it to Joe.

Seb and I both look at the rock Helen just mounted.

Seb turns to me. 'Shall we?'

'Go on then!' I laugh.

We climb up onto the rock. The sun has lowered even deeper in the sky and the lights is even softer, a deeper golden shade. Seb puts his arm around me and we smile at the camera. He plants a kiss on my head, and I laugh. Joe takes a few pictures. I realise, even in this fleeting moment, that I'm happy up here on this mountain with him. I'm always happy when I'm with Seb. He just makes everything feel okay. He draws a side out of me that had been dormant for ages until I met him. An adventurous side, a free-spiritedness, a love for life. I don't want to lose him. I really don't.

'Got some great shots!' Joe says.

'Thanks Joe,' I reply as I jump off the rock.

Joe hands my camera back.

'Any time,' he says.

I'm realising that despite Joe and Cody's competitive bravado around each other, Joe is actually quite sweet and sensitive. He seems to be observant too, aware of everyone's mood. I hadn't even realised having a picture with Seb might be what I needed in that particular moment, but Joe seemed to sense it. I scroll through the pictures and find that there are some gems.

'These are perfect!' I gush, realising I sound just like Helen.

Unlike Helen, neither Seb or myself are particularly active on social media. I glance over at her to see her looking glumly my way. Realising I'm looking, she quickly corrects her expression and fixes on a smile. I show the pictures to Seb, who is equally pleased with them.

'Do you guys want photos taken too?' I ask Joe and Cody.

'No, I'm okay. I'm starving,' Joe says.

'Same!' Cody echoes. 'I could eat a horse. Or a yak.'

We laugh weakly and continue down the path towards the guesthouse.

13 CHAPTER THIRTEEN

The owner of our new guesthouse is a lot less friendly than Hanka and seems tired and weary of travellers. She greets us with a curt 'hello' and shows us to our rooms, explaining that dinner will be ready in half an hour. The room is basic to say the least. In fact, it feels more like a cattle shed, with stone walls and two small rickety twin beds. There's no furniture to speak of and just a bulb dangling from the ceiling.

'They just get better and better!' I groan.

'Mmm, not exactly cosy!' Seb pulls a face.

He lies down on one of the beds. 'I'm so knackered I could sleep anywhere though,' he says.

'I know what you mean,' I reply, sitting on the edge of the other bed and untying the laces of my hiking boots.

I pull them off and inspect my blisters. A few of the plasters I put on earlier have come off, revealing the red, swollen blisters underneath. I put some new plasters on and then lie back on the bed, letting out a sigh of relief. Although the trip is proving pretty gruelling, I have to admit that there is something quite calming about so much walking. The physical exertion is grounding and even though the worries about my and Seb's relationship remain, they don't feel as overwhelming as before. I feel less bothered about the bigger picture and more content to simply be in the here and now.

'Do you think I can fit a shower in before dinner?' I ask Seb.

'Yeah, go for it,' he says.

I get up, find my towel and toiletries from my bag and get undressed, before wrapping a towel around my body and heading to the shower room next to our room. As expected, it's not exactly plush: a loosely tiled cubicle with nothing but a showerhead and a drain. A spider crawls across the floor and slips into the plughole. I shudder, but step tentatively into the cubicle. It's not like I have any choice. There aren't exactly going to be other, fancier, bathrooms around.

I turn on the shower and fortunately, the water is nice and warm. I stand under the hot stream, looking nervously at the plughole, hoping the spider doesn't reappear. I think about my friends and family as I wash the sweat off my body and the traces of blood from my legs where the leeches attached themselves earlier. I need to let my parents know how I'm doing soon. My parents lead a quiet life and tend not to stray more than a few miles from their house in Surrey. They're homebodies and watch a variety of soaps religiously - Emmerdale, Coronation Street and EastEnders, I think they even dabble in Hollyoaks. My mum's the kind of person who's on first name terms with the postman, she asks after the kids of the owner of the local newsagent and she's in the same book group as her GP. My dad's not quite as outgoing as she is. He's disabled and so spends more time at home. I'm close to my parents and they tend to be supportive of what I do, even though when I moved to London, my mum kept forwarding me articles about pollution and crime rates every week for the first six months. In the end, she accepted my choice to live in the crime-infested capital and focus on my career, but I think both my parents are beginning to get a bit worried about me now. My mum mentioned how one of my cousins had got married recently during our last phone call, describing the wedding as 'beautiful', 'a truly moving day'. Her voice sounding full of emotion. I felt a bit down after the call, as though I should be having a beautiful or moving day too. Even though I've made a conscious effort to abandon my Life List and focus on authentic happiness instead, rather than ticking life goals off a checklist, that conversation did get to me a bit. I know my mum thinks it's exciting that I'm in Nepal, climbing Everest, hiking and meeting new people, but her enthusiasm is a little forced. I think she'd much rather I was planning a wedding, or shopping for a dress.

I sigh, rinsing the soap suds off my limbs. I push the uneasy thoughts out of my mind and shampoo my hair, listening to the sound of birds in the trees outside. I turn the shower off and wrap my towel around me. I peer out of the shower room, check there's no one along the corridor, and then make a dash to mine and Seb's room. As I open the door, I see he's having a video call on his iPad.

'Just talking to my dad,' he says in a hushed voice over the top of his iPad.

I nod. Staying out of shot of the camera, I wrap my wet hair in a towel and put on some underwear and comfy old jogging bottoms, crumpled from having been at the bottom of my backpack. I run a comb through my hair and drape a towel around my shoulders. I perch on the edge of my bed and dry my hair.

'Yeah, we did twenty kilometres today, got to an altitude of 5,600 metres,' Seb tells his dad.

'Five thousand six hundred? When I scaled Everest, we got to 8,850,' Greg fires back.

I roll my eyes, irritated. Here Greg goes, always trying to compete with Seb. Why can't he just let Seb be? Why does he always have to one-up him?

'Well, we're only on the first day!' Seb reminds him.

'I know. You'll make better progress soon,' Greg assures him.

I flinch and reach over across the small space between mine and Seb's beds to squeeze his knee. I give him a sympathetic look and he smiles back weakly.

'Rachel's here,' he says.

I fix a smile onto my face as Seb tilts the iPad towards me.

'Hi Greg!' I wave, smiling politely.

'Hey Rachel!' Seb's dad waves back, flashing me a charming smile.

Greg is attractive for an older man, but he has more of a preppy look than Seb, with whitened teeth, neat, gelled-back hair, and a penchant for rugby shirts, which cling to his broad, thickly-muscled chest.

His eyes linger for a beat too long on my make-up free face and wet hair, and I realise this is the first time he's seen me au naturel. Will he find me lacking too, like he seems to find his son? I smile self-consciously.

'Just got out of the shower, huh?' he says.

'Yep,' I reply.

'Great! Must feel good after all the exercise,' he comments.

'Yes, definitely,' I reply, frowning slightly.

Is he implying that I don't normally exercise? I don't, but that's not the point. I decide not to dwell on it and push the thought out of my mind.

'It's beautiful up here. Stunning. But of course, you know that,' I comment.

'Oh yeah, it's wonderful. It gets better the higher up the mountain you get. You'll find out, if you can hack the altitude sickness!' Greg says with a cheeky grin.

'I'm sure we can handle it,' I reply with a bright smile that hides the prickling defensiveness I'm feeling.

We came to Everest to have fun. It's not a competition, and yet Greg is making out like it is, clinging to his Everest glory from 30 years ago.

'It can be tough. It's not for the faint-hearted!'' he continues.

'Oh well, we're up for the challenge!' I insist, my voice a little tight.

'That's a fighting spirit you've got there, Rachel!' Greg laughs. 'But it's difficult. See if you're still feeling this way in a few days' time.'

Seb smiles awkwardly.

'We know it's not going to be easy. We already have blisters and we've been bitten by leeches and yet we're still up for it. We can do it!' Seb insists, sounding a little defensive now too.

'Yeah, we can,' I add, smiling at him, feeling proud that he's standing up to his dad for once.

'Leeches? Blisters? Already! Yeesh!' Greg pulls a face. 'When I climbed Everest, we had this ingenious trick for avoiding blisters,' Greg says, before launching into some explanation of how he and his fellow hiking buddies would put baby powder in their socks to avoid rubbing. It sounds like a pretty good idea, but it's not exactly much use to us now that we're already up Everest. I doubt the local chai seller stocks baby powder and I'm pretty sure Amazon Prime don't deliver.

'Great,' Seb replies, sounding a bit exasperated.

I look at the time on his iPad and realise we've been away for thirty-five minutes when dinner was meant to be ready after half an hour. I point at the time and give Seb a look, while his dad drones on about baby powder.

'Dad, we have to go. The guesthouse is serving dinner now,' Seb explains, cutting his dad off.

I brace myself for Greg to make some mean comment about how when he climbed Everest, he hunted wild boar or something like that, but fortunately, he spares us.

'Alright son, well, have a good one. Good luck with the rest of the hike,' he says.

'Thanks dad, speak soon,' Seb replies.

He ends the call and lets out a long sigh of relief. I roll my eyes dramatically.

'How do you put up with that?' I ask.

'He's not that bad,' Seb replies weakly.

'Really?' I reply, raising an eyebrow.

'He's just re-living his hey-dey,' Seb comments.

'Hmm…' I murmur.

'How was your shower?' he asks, changing the subject.

I get the feeling he doesn't want me to be negative about his dad so I let it go even though I wish Seb would do what feels right for him rather than trying to please his dad all the time.

'It was nice,' I reply.

'Good,' he says, with a smile that almost conceals the look of sadness in his eyes.

14 CHAPTER FOURTEEN

I really, really hate to say this, but Seb's dad might have been right. It's almost like the first day of the Everest trail was just a taster, getting us used to things. The second day is proving so much harder. The nice, winding mountain paths have been replaced by a rough, rocky terrain that we've had to pick our way over, using walking sticks. It's not just a little bit rocky; the terrain is made up of huge clusters with jagged edges that require you to choose where you're stepping with precision, so you don't trip up and fall, risking slicing your ankles on some sharp edges. It takes so much concentration that it's hard to talk and even though we tried to chat at first, conversation soon died down. Even Cody and Joe, who tend to spend most of the trek comparing their step count and tracking the altitude, stop talking, concentrating on the uneven jagged rocks instead. The terrain was like that for hours, but the perk was the view of the mountains. The sky has been a bright blue all day, the sun beaming down and glowing off the snow-capped mountains. Handling the rough terrain has been exhausting and challenging, but the scenery has been epic, even if my blisters have rubbed a bit.

Making it across miles and miles of rocks, we arrive at a mountain café tucked away and drink chai like it's the most delicious thing ever. We devour momos and dishes of rice and vegetables. They're the kind of unremarkable dishes that would seem far too basic at any restaurant anywhere else, but here on the Everest trail are perfect. We need carbs and vegetables, healthy fuel. And the hunger caused by so much walking makes everything taste incredible anyway.

We demolish our food, pretty much in silence and then sit back, drinking chai. The owner of the café, a woman called Chana, tells us how she and her husband have been married for fifty years and grew up in a small village not too far away. Apparently, she and her husband, Ragav, would play together as children. Her husband's family moved away when he was around ten years old and she thought she'd never see him again. She moved to Kathmandu to work for a textiles company and she was in the post office one day, sending a letter home, when Ragav walked in. It turned out he lived on the same road as her. Fate had brought them back together and they ended up falling in love. The story is so adorable and even though I expect she's told it many times to tourists doing this trek, her eyes still sparkle as relays it now. She refills our cups of chai and then goes to greet another group of walkers who have just arrived. As we reflect on Chana's story of her one true love, conversation between us moves on to relationships.

Cody recalls his first love: a guy he met when he was a teenager. It turns out they met in the cutest way. A friend pulled out of a gig he and Cody were meant to be going to and so Cody advertised the spare gig ticket on eBay. Someone offered to buy it and they arranged to meet outside the concert venue, except when Cody handed over the ticket, the guy invited him to hang out with him and his friends, and they ended up spending the whole night together, laughing, joking, flirting and dancing, and then they stayed together for three years.

'Oh my God, that's adorable!' I gush, even though I'm reeling slightly from the news that Cody is gay. It hadn't occurred to me at all.

'Yeah, I got lucky that night for sure,' Cody says, smiling.

'I'm going to try it next time I'm single,' I suggest. 'Whack a gig ticket on eBay, sell it to the hottest-sounding bidder!'

Cody laughs. 'Probably better than Tinder!'

'Hey, what do you mean "next time you're single"?' Seb protests, pouting with mock petulance.

I grin. 'Only joking,' I reply, leaning into him.

'What about you Helen, any epic romances?' Joe asks.

'Oh, not really.' Helen shrugs. She takes a sip of chai.

'At least no big monogamous romances like the kind you're talking about. I don't believe there's just one soulmate for us in this life,' she says. 'I believe you can fall in love many times, with many people, if your heart is open. I don't really believe people are designed for long term monogamy.' She glances at Seb.

I roll my eyes.

'I just think monogamy is a bit like religion,' Helen comments. 'Times have changed. I like the quote, "Love is cursed by monogamy".'

'Who said that?' Seb asks.

'Kanye West,' Helen replies.

We all laugh, having assumed she was quoting some spiritual leader.

'I don't think monogamy is a curse,' I comment. 'Deciding that you're going to be true to one person and be in it for the long-haul, resist temptation and just commit, sticking by someone's side through all the highs and lows and the journey of life... I can't think of anything more romantic.'

Seb squeezes my hand under the table.

Helen shrugs. 'Each to their own.'

'So have you had any holiday romances then Helen?' Joe asks.

'No! Not really, but if love were to come my way, I'd certainly be open to it,' Helen comments, holding his gaze.

I clear my throat.

'Well, good luck with that Helen,' I reply in a firm voice.

Joe lets out a little laugh and Helen shoots him a look. He and I exchange a sly smile.

'What about you, Joe? Are you seeing anyone?' I ask, wondering in the back of my mind whether he and Helen might be a good match. Joe's not a bad-looking guy by any means. He looks a bit like Jude Law crossed with Chris Hemsworth. He's got a tan, blue eyes, muscles, and the way he wears his hair in a tousled man bun is kind of sexy. Even I can see that. Helen would be lucky to have someone like him.

'Oh, no, I'm not seeing anyone,' Joe replies, smiling awkwardly and glancing down at the table.

'Oh ok.' I raise an eyebrow at Seb, wondering why Joe's acting so awkwardly.

Seb raises an eyebrow back.

'Any holiday romances?' I ask.

A flush instantly appears on Joe's neck and face and I find myself immediately regretting the question.

'No! Romance isn't really my thing at the moment,' he says, shrugging. 'I'm just relaxing, chilling, going with the flow.'

Cody coughs.

'Fair enough,' I reply. 'Taking a break can be a really good thing. I split up with my ex before I came to India. Well, actually I followed him to India thinking I could win him back, but then when I got here, I did some soul-searching and realised I was actually okay on my own. I'd wanted to get married by 30, but then I found myself 31 and single and found that actually, it wasn't so bad!'

'And I took a celibacy pledge for a year,' Seb adds. 'No sex, at all. I just wanted to cut out all those distractions and focus on me.'

Joe nods.

'A year?!' Helen balks. 'That must have been impossible!'

'Well, it was pretty tough,' Seb admits. 'I screwed up once when I went to see a friend for his birthday in Thailand, then I was pretty good for a few months, but then I met Rachel,' Seb explains, giving me a conspiratorial smile.

'Oh, right!' Helen replies, shifting in her seat. 'It's a shame you didn't complete it. Just think of all the nuggets of wisdom you might be missing out on.'

I laugh. 'I think he's alright as he is, Helen!'

'I know!' she replies innocently. 'But you never know, he might have been Shiva reincarnate if he'd carried on!'

Seb and I exchange a look. He smiles awkwardly.

'Oh well, I think he enjoyed being corrupted in the end, didn't you, Seb?' I say, nudging him.

'Yeah, I'm not complaining! Wisdom shmisdom!' Seb grins.

We all laugh, except Helen, who mutters something about wisdom being 'really important, actually'.

'I've heard from a lot of people that monogamy is really constrictive when you actually think about it. We're just conditioned to want these long-term exclusive relationships, but they're so restrictive,' Helen says. 'I think if we actually connected with ourselves and let our hearts be open, we'd all be a lot happier.'

'Uh-huh,' I reply weakly.

Joe, Cody and Seb have a similar response, barely listening to Helen as we finish our chai and settle our bill, before setting off on the next leg of our trek, an 8-kilometre stretch. The terrain is meant to be less intense as earlier, the rocky stretches replaced by winding paths.

We walk for five minutes, the path gentle and relaxing. Although it's hot, the sun burning in the sky.

'God, I am boiling!' Helen says, exasperatedly.

'One second guys,' she says, stopping by a boulder.

We all pause as she heaves off her backpack, leaving it on the boulder. She then grips the hem of her top and peels it off, revealing a cropped top underneath that I'm not sure counts as outerwear of underwear. I feel like my eyes are bulging as I take in her taught slim body. Not an ounce of fat. I can't help feeling a tiny bit insecure. I scoff a bit at yoga, but clearly it's working for her.

She ties her top around her waist and fans herself with her hands.

'Helen, this is a conservative country,' Cody reminds her.

'I know, I'm just too hot,' she says.

'It is hot,' Cody admits.

He's wearing nothing but a baggy vest that hands loosely over his muscles.

'Yeah, it's pretty boiling,' I comment, feeling frumpy in my baggy T-shirt.

I could take it off, but I'm not wearing a sports bra underneath, I'm wearing a regular white bra and I doubt the locals of Nepal would appreciate seeing me in it.

Helen unzips a side pocket of her backpack and retrieves a tube of sun cream. She squirts some onto her hand and starts rubbing it onto her arms, stomach and shoulders.

'I can't reach my back,' she grumbles. 'Can someone help?'

She looks instantly at Seb and hands him the sun cream, her eyes latching onto his.

'Err…' Seb hesitates. 'Okay,' he replies.

I feel a twinge of unease. It's one thing that Helen looks has been preaching about how unnatural monogamy is, but now she wants Seb to rub lotion into her near naked top half? No, I'm not having it.

'I'll do it! I have a great, err, moisturising technique!' I insist, stepping in and taking the sun cream off Seb.

A flicker of disappointment passes over Helen's face, letting me know that her intentions in asking Seb to apply her sun cream her weren't entirely innocent.

'Turn around,' I order her, my irritation coming through in my voice.

She turns around and I apply the sun cream. I catch Seb's eye and he raises an eyebrow, smirking slightly. I roll my eyes and finish off rubbing the sun cream into Helen's skin.

'There you go, all done,' I say.

She turns around.

'Great moisturising technique!' she jokes, a sarcastic tone to her voice.

'I know,' I comment.

I hand her the cream and she zips it back into her backpack pocket, puts her backpack on, and we carry on with the walk. The terrain is so much less taxing and Seb and I amble along, dropping back from the others slightly.

'God, Helen is ridiculous,' I scoff, once Seb and I are out of earshot. I clamber over some rocks in our path. 'Acting like you've missed out on your spiritual quest because of me!' I exclaim breathily.

Seb laughs, shaking his head. 'Yeah, she's pretty intense!'

'Could she be any more obvious?! Wanting you to apply lotion to her? And all that rubbish she was spouting… "I believe your heart should be open. Monogamy isn't natural",' I parrot in a catty American accent.

'I know. It is a bit awkward,' Seb says, finally admitting it. He reaches for my hand and helps me over some rocks in the path. We walk on together, holding hands.

I laugh. 'That's one way of putting it! At least you finally see that this is not just normal Canadian friendliness!' I comment.

'No, it's definitely a bit more than just friendliness,' Seb says.

'A lot more,' I sigh. 'She flirts with you like I'm not even in the room!'

'I know!' Seb comments. 'It's pretty brazen.'

'Very brazen,' I remark, as a man with a donkey passes us on the path.

We smile and say hello. I find myself hoping Cody didn't say "yak attack" as usual as the man passed him, before he got to us. But he looks unfazed and simply smiles before continuing down the path.

'I don't know why Helen can't just go for Joe,' I grumble as we pass through an alcove of trees.

'Yeah, well, maybe she just doesn't think he has my charm,' Seb jokes, grinning mischievously.

I roll my eyes indulgently. 'One in a million, aren't you?'

'Damn straight,' Seb comments, grinning.

'But seriously, Joe's good-looking, he's sweet, he's sensitive,' I remark. 'He has that tousled blonde man bun, the muscles…'

Seb raises an eyebrow. 'Sounds like you might have a crush on Joe,' he teases. 'Maybe you should go for him and I'll go for Helen.'

I shoot him a look. 'Not funny.'

Seb grins.

'I'm just saying, he's a good-looking guy and single. Unlike you. Why can't she just go for him?'

'Like I said, irresistible!' Seb grins.

'Honestly!' I tut, rolling me eyes.

We come out of the shadowy passageway and emerge at another point along the mountain, where the view is unbroken by trees and the sun melts behind the snow-capped mountains in the distance. We both stand still, awe-struck by how beautiful it is. The sky is adorned with wispy clouds that glow pink in the low sun, Everest soaring amongst them. It's a truly jaw-dropping sight.

'Wow,' I utter, taking Seb's hand. I rest my head on his shoulder and lean into him. He puts his arm around me, pulling me close.

The sun dips lower behind the mountains.

'I know this is a really cheesy moment to say this, but I love you, Rachel. I really do,' Seb says, his voice cracking with emotion.

I gaze up at him, into his kind familiar eyes, and smile.

'I love you too Seb,' I tell him.

Suddenly a cry from Cody pierces the moment.

'Yak attack!'

Seb and I both laugh as we see Cody dodging another donkey in the distance.

15 CHAPTER FIFTEEN

I feel exhausted by the time we arrive at the guesthouse. The hiking has taken it out of me and I feel quite irritated by Helen's brazen flirting with Seb, but I try to put it out of my mind. I don't want to let her ruin our adventure here in Nepal.

Fortunately, the guesthouse we're staying at is a bit nicer than the previous two, with comfier beds and a cosy room that's nicely decorated and even has a bit of furniture. The WiFi signal is good too and I check my messages. I have one from Meera.

Can you call me? There's something I want to talk to you about.

Hmm. That's weird.

I turn to Seb, who is putting fresh plasters on a couple of blisters adorning his feet.

'I just got this message from Meera saying there's something she wants to talk to me about,' I tell him. 'What do you think it could be?'

Seb frowns. 'I don't know… Call her, it might be something serious.'

'Yeah, you're right.'

I click onto WhatsApp and call Meera, hoping she'll pick up. She answers after a few rings.

'Hey!' she says, sounding happy to hear from me. 'How are

you? How's the trek? Glad you're still alive!' She laughs.

'Just about! Although Seb is bandaging up blisters right now!'

'Eww!' Meera grimaces.

'How are you? How are the babies?' I ask.

'Oh, it's intense!' Meera comments. 'They're waking up every few hours during the night. One goes down and then the other decides to scream. But Fred and I are taking it in turns to look after them. He does one night, and I do the other so we at least get some sleep.'

'Woah! It does sound intense!'

'It is, but they're adorable, Rachel. I can't stop looking at them. Wait, let me video call you!'

Meera hangs up and video calls me instead. She looks tired, eyebags adorning her usually flawless complexion and her hair, which is always sleek and brushed hangs in messy curtains. But she's smiling and her eyes are sparkling.

'Look at my little angels!' she exclaims, turning the camera towards two tiny little babies lying in baby chairs. One of them is fast asleep and the other is blinking and gurgling. They're both totally adorable.

'Aww!' I gush. 'They're so cute!'

'I know, right? I can't believe I made them!' Meera gushes.

We chat a bit more about the highs and lows of motherhood, before Meera suddenly looks more serious.

'There's something I wanted to talk to you about,' she says.

'What's that?' I ask, feeling a little on edge. What could it possibly be?

'Is Seb there?' Meera asks.

'Yeah, one second.'

I beckon Seb over.

'Hey Meera!' he says, waving at the screen.

'Hey Seb,' she replies, smiling, despite still looking a bit tense.

'What is it, Meera?'

'Well, Fred and I were wondering if you and Seb might

consider, erm…' She pauses.

Seb and I exchange a baffled look.

'We were wondering if you and Seb might consider being, erm, godparents to Ajay and Azar,' she says. 'I know we haven't known each other for that long, but I feel a connection with you two. I have so many people passing through the guesthouse every day, but I rarely bond with people like I did with you guys. You two became like family to me and I'd just really like you to be like family to my little boys too.'

Meera smiles sweetly.

'Oh my God!' I utter, feeling completely shocked.

I had not seen that coming at all.

'We'd love to!' I gush. 'Well, I'd love to! Seb?'

I turn to Seb who looks as delighted and touched as I feel.

'I'd love to as well! It would be an honour, Meera! Wow!' Seb gushes.

Meera's face lights up. 'I'm so happy you said yes!' she says. 'I'm so relieved. I was worried you'd think it was too much!'

'Of course not. I'm so happy you asked us! Wow!' I exclaim.

'Oh, thank you guys! Do you want to see your godchildren again?' Meera asks, grinning.

'Of course!' I reply.

Meera points her phone towards Ajay and Azar and my heart melts. I reach for Seb's hand and we exchange a soppy smile. We're godparents to these beautiful kids.

Suddenly Azar scrunches up his face and starts bawling.

'Oh guys, don't take it personally but he just did a poo!' Meera laughs.

Seb and I crack up as Meera says goodbye, needing to go and change Azar's nappy.

'Speak soon godmother and godfather!' Meera says.

'Speak soon! Bye godchildren!' I reply, waving at my little godchildren on the screen.

'Bye Ajay. Bye Azar,' Seb says.

We hang up and I turn to Seb, full of emotion.

'I can't believe it! We're godparents!'

To my surprise, Seb looks really emotional, his eyes moist.

'I can't believe it either!' he croaks.

'Aww!' I stroke his arm, surprised by just how moved he is.

'I never thought something like this would happen to me!' he says. 'I can't believe it. When I came to India, I felt like the worst person, just a toxic mess, and now someone wants me to be godparent to their children.'

Seb shakes his head in disbelief, his eyes brimming with emotion. When he first came to India, he was wracked with guilt because he'd had a fling with a tourist at the ski resort he was working at and she'd ended up pregnant. She decided to have an abortion and really struggled with it, suffering from depression. Seb blamed himself for the whole thing and felt it was a wake-up call to do some soul-searching. Fortunately, the woman, Vanessa, started feeling much happier. She got a boyfriend and got pregnant, decided to keep her baby, and Seb moved on, but there's clearly still a part of him that feels raw and vulnerable from the experience.

'Seb, you're going to make an amazing godparent. You're kind, caring, smart and wise. Of course, Meera would want you to be a godfather to Ajay and Azar,' I reassure him.

'I just… If you'd told me this six months ago, I'd never have believed you,' Seb says.

I smile. 'I wouldn't have thought I'd be a godparent either,' I admit. 'But we're both come a long way.'

'Yeah, I guess we have. Come here,' Seb says, beckoning me towards him.

I snuggle into him as he wraps his arms around me.

16 CHAPTER SIXTEEN

I'm in a great mood all day. Maybe it's because of Meera's news or maybe it's because the hike has been easy today with no more jutting rocks to clamber over. The weather is perfect, sunny but with a cool breeze. I've taken loads of photos and keep finding myself gazing off into the distance, admiring the rugged snow-capped mountains. A stream flows alongside our path, making a soothing gushing noise. Birds chirp in the trees and it occurs to me that the sounds of nature are so relaxing and vivid up here that they remind me of the type of background music you get in spas. Our footsteps are the only interruption from the ambience. The path veers around a bend and the view unfolds even more, revealing an even more stunning panorama of mountain peaks, and then I spot a bridge, draped flimsily between two mountains. My stomach lurches – the momentarily zen I'd been feeling instantly replaced by dread. Not another flimsy bridge. This one is far longer than any of the others we've crossed so far and it's far higher up. I feel my toes curl just looking at it. So much for my great mood!

Seb must be reading my thoughts as he turns and catches my eye.

'You can do it,' he reassures me.

I shake my head, still unable to quite process just how high up this bridge is. Cody, Joe and Helen march confidently towards it, like it's a pavement. They look completely unfazed.

I mean, technically, I can cross the bridge, It's not exactly rocket science. I can put one foot in front of the other and walk, I just don't like doing things that are clearly unsafe. The bridge looks so flimsy. I've never had appreciation for English heavy-handed health and safety regulations like I do right now. I mean, who checks these bridges? Is there any form of maintenance or do they just get replaced once they break and some sad unfortunate soul plunges to their death? I don't want to be that person! And I could well be given the way Cody and Joe plough across these bridges like they're invincible.

I sigh, feeling a bit irritated by Seb's encouragement. Just because you can do something, doesn't mean you should. I don't need to prove to myself that I can walk across a flimsy bridge thousands of metres up a mountain.

'Oh man, this one looks like the craziest bridge yet!' Cody enthuses, grinning.

'Woah, this one is mad!' Joe concurs, looking just as excited.

I glance at Helen. She frowns at the bridge, hanging back a little. Even she seems a bit unnerved by this one.

'Dude, did you hear about that Australian girl who fell off a suspension bridge in Pakistan?' Cody says, turning to Joe. 'She fell into a river and got swept along in the currents for twenty kilometres. Nearly died.'

'Err, Cody, that's not particular helpful right now,' Seb comments, shooting Cody a look.

Cody glances at me and takes in my no doubt white fraught face.

'Oh yeah. Sorry Rachel. It was just a one off. And that bridge was nothing like this one. This one's way better,' Cody insists, smiling awkwardly.

'Mmm-hmm,' I reply.

Seb rubs my back.

I find myself daydreaming once more about my house in

London. My cosy sofa - a gorgeous red velvet Chesterfield one I spent far too much money on. I wish I was there right now, snuggled up, safe.

We pass under some trees, their branches entwining above our heads to form a canopy, dappled light falling through. Rain from last night's storm still clings to the branches and falls onto us, a gentle spattering, as we pass through, the branches shaking as Cody and Joe barrel forward.

'This is cute,' I comment, admiring the passageway, while trying not to think about what's on the other side. 'If only the whole trek could be like this!'

'Yeah,' Seb concurs, but I can tell he doesn't really mean it.

Like Cody and Joe, he's charging ahead, seeming eager to get to the bridge. What is with men and this daredevil shit? I wipe raindrops from my forehead as we emerge. The bridge isn't far ahead now. It looks really flimsy. It's got wire handrails and rickety planks shoddily constructed with gaps between them. It's suspended across a plunging ravine, thousands and thousands of metres deep. Oh God. This is going to be the bridge that finishes me. I picture the headlines in the papers back home: 'London lawyer plunges to her death in Nepal', or, 'British tourist dies in tragic fall on Everest trek'. I do not want to cross this bridge.

'Oh man, this is like something out of a film!' Cody comments, wide-eyed as he takes in the long precarious length of it.

'Yeah, a film where everyone dies,' I add.

Cody laughs and lets out a 'whoop', his voice echoing around the mountains.

He barrels towards the bridge and pauses just before he steps onto it. For a moment, I start to wonder if he's having second thoughts.

'Holy shit guys! Look at how high up we are!' he says, peering down at the drop below.

He's so close to the edge that it makes my palms sweat just to look at him. I think of Tube stations in London and how the TfL loudspeaker always warns: stand back from the yellow line. If there were yellow lines on mountain edges, Cody would have definitely crossed them.

We approach the bridge, and the others join Cody in peering down at the drop below.

'Woah!' Seb utters.

Joe stands by Cody's side and gazes down into the abyss below, more with interest and awe than fear. I linger behind them. I can't even bring myself to look.

'Let's go, guys!' Cody says, fist pumping the air, before charging across the bridge.

I gasp as it creaks and sways under his weight. Even Helen and Seb gasp, eyes wide. Joe also looks on, a little fretfully.

'Wooooohhh!' Cody cries out, holding his arms out, looking at the mountain ranges all around him. 'Yeah, man! This is the life!'

Joe hollers back at him.

'Somebody take my photo!' Cody shouts.

He turns around and holds his arms out wide, like he's on top of the world, which bar reaching the actual peak of Everest, he pretty much is. More headlines scroll through my mind: New York man found dead in Himilaya horror fall, Tragedy as personal trainer dies in Everest base camp trek, Last photo of traveller taken seconds before fatal fall.

Joe takes the camera that's dangling around his neck and stands at the end of the bridge, trying to frame the perfect photo, while Cody continues to pose, arms in the air. The sight of him, posing, not even holding onto the rails of the bridge, gives me vertigo. I look away.

'You got it?' Cody shouts.

'Yeah!' Joe replies, giving Cody the thumbs up.

Turning off his camera, Joe steps fearlessly onto the bridge and starts walking across. The bridge bobs up and down as he and Cody make their way across it.

'How are they so relaxed?' I comment as the bridge sighs and creaks.

Cody bounds towards the other side and lets out another victorious yelp as he reaches land again, clearly high on adrenaline. Joe quickens his pace, not stopping for a picture. He crosses the bridge unfazed as Helen, Seb and I look on. He reaches the other side, joining Cody.

The bridge is empty.

Helen shrugs.

'I guess you've just got to go for it!' she says, stepping forward onto the bridge.

She starts out a little tentative but after a few steps, she's sauntering across, treating the bridge like a runway.

Great. So Helen isn't afraid of death trap bridges. Typical.

'Seb,' I mutter, 'I really don't think that's safe – I mean look at it. Can't we go another way?' I look back down the path we've come.

'There is no other way,' Seb says. 'We'll just end up going backwards.'

Backwards sounds pretty appealing right now.

'Yeah, but…' I look back to the bridge, swaying, as Helen walks jauntily across.

'Maybe we should go back. I mean… I…'

Seb frowns.

'I don't want to die,' I point out.

'You're not going to die!' Seb laughs, rolling his eyes.

'Famous last words! People do die doing stuff like this Seb. We're not invincible just because we act that way. We could easily die! It's like getting an illness or something, you never think it's going to happen to you or someone you love and then it does, you know…'

I realise I'm rambling. It's the nerves.

Seb smiles, his expression both perplexed and sympathetic.

'I guess so, but I just don't think we're going to die crossing this bridge. If it was so unsafe, it wouldn't be here. They'd have had to remove it. Thousands of people cross this bridge every year,' Seb comments.

'I know, but what if the bridge is on its last legs? You never know when it might collapse. You or I could be that one person – the straw that breaks the camel's back. The unlucky tourists who went tumbling into the abyss, a footnote in the history of Everest. We might be the tourists who lost their lives to remind locals that they need a better bridge. We might end up dying for the sake of future generations' bridge safety. I don't want my legacy to be a safe bridge,' I insist.

'I think you're overthinking this,' Seb remarks, his lips curling into a smile. 'Your legacy isn't going to be a bridge. It's not as flimsy as it looks.'

To illustrate his point, Seb grabs the side of the bridge and shakes it, causing a ripple effect that makes the bridge wobble.

'It's actually quite sturdy,' he says, looking down at the handrails. 'These are reinforced with metal.'

He's right. There is some metal woven into the rails, but I still don't feel reassured. My heart pounds in my chest. My palms sweat.

'Oh God,' I utter.

'Come on, it'll be fine. Just one foot in front of the other. We'll go slow, treading carefully. We won't pound it like Cody did. If we walk across it gently. It'll be fine,' Seb insists.

'Urghh,' I grumble.

Seb gives me an encouraging smile.

'Guys! Come on!' Cody shouts across the abyss. 'What are you waiting for?'

'We're coming!' Seb shouts back.

'Speak for yourself!' I huff to Seb.

Seb reaches over and takes my hands in his. He fixes me with a serious look.

'We can do this, Rachel. Just one step in front of the other. It'll be okay.'

I look into his tender, sincere eyes. I've always found Seb's eyes so reassuring. I've lost track of the number of times I've gazed into them when stressed or upset and felt calmer and happier. I think I've become somewhat hard-wired to find his eyes relaxing and in spite of myself, I feel the panic in my chest abate somewhat.

'We're going to be okay. I know it's scary, but we'll make it,' he assures me in a measured tone.

'Okay, okay, I'll do it,' I grumble, giving in.

Seb smiles. 'Do you want to go first or shall I?' he asks.

'I don't know. I guess I'll go first,' I say, liking the idea of Seb behind me.

'Okay, cool,' Seb says, with a reassuring smile. 'You go and I'll follow in a few minutes. We don't want to put too much pressure on the bridge at once.'

'Okay,' I reply, gulping.

I step towards the bridge and look down, feeling anxiety flare up in my chest as I take in the vast drop.

'Don't look down. Just think of it as a normal walk. One step in front of the other, walking steadily across,' Seb suggests. 'Don't overthink it. Just walk.'

'Okay,' I reply.

I take a deep breath and try not to think about the drop below. I try to clear my mind of all thoughts and do what Seb said – just walk. I take a step onto the bridge. It creaks and dips under my feet.

'Oh God. This is nothing like a normal walk,' I croak.

'Gently does it. Don't overthink it. One step in front of the other. You can do this,' Seb assures me.

I take another step forward and then another. The bridge sways and creaks as I move. My sofa back in London flashes through my mind again. I want to be there. So badly. My limbs feel stiff, like they're locking with fear.

'Seb, this is terrifying,' I utter.

'Keep going. Deep breaths,' Seb says.

'Okay.'

I take a few deep breaths and put one foot in front of the other. I keep walking, even though my legs are so stiff that I feel like I'm wading through sinking sand. My hands are drenched in sweat and are so slick that my grip on the sides of the bridge feels slippery and loose. I look ahead at Cody, Joe and Helen, waiting for me on the other side. Helen has got her camera out and is taking a photo. A photo?! How can she take a picture of me right now, in my most stressful, excruciating moment? Can she not see that I'm a nervous wreck? This is not an insta-worthy moment, for goodness sake. I want to shout across at her to put the camera down but I'm too far away and I'm so paralyzed by fear that I can't quite bring myself to shout. Great, just great. Now my most unnerving moment is on record. Helen will probably put the pictures up on Instagram later and tag me.

I look away, trying not to focus on what she's doing and trying not to get distracted, but in doing so, I stupidly look downwards, and glimpse the vast abyss beneath me. Oh God. The bridge is wobbling, and I realise I'm shaking, trembling like a leaf. My hands are quivering, rattling against the bridge.

'Seb,' I utter. 'I don't know if I can do this.'

'You can do it,' Seb insists, although he doesn't sound particularly sure anymore either. 'Just keep walking.'

'I want to turn around,' I say, looking over my shoulder. The bridge is so narrow that it would be near impossible to turn while wearing my backpack and I'd have to take my hands off the handles if I were to take it off. Oh God. I'm stuck.

'You can do this, Rachel. Just look ahead and walk. One foot in front of the other,' Seb says.

'Okay,' I reply, realising that I'm halfway along the bridge anyway. If I turn around and head back, I'll still have just the same number of steps going back that I would to get to the other side.

I can do this, I try to tell myself. I can do it. Just one foot in front of the other. Just keep going. One step and then another step, and then eventually I'll be on land and this will all be over. I take another few tentative steps, keeping my eyes focused on some trees on the other side of the mountain, to the left of Cody, Joe and Helen. I think Helen is still taking my picture, but I don't care. I'm not going to focus on her right now. I'll just insist she deletes whatever she's taken later.

One step. Another step. The bridge is swaying a little bit, but I'm making progress. I can do this. The trees are coming closer into sight.

All of a sudden, I feel a stinging sensation on my calf. What the hell?! I try to block it out. I don't want to look down again in case I catch sight of the vast drop below and start shaking even more, and yet the pain is sharp and insistent. What is this?!

I brave it and look down, only to see a leech – an enormous leech, the biggest leech I've seen - has attached itself to my calf and is greedily gulping up my blood. A trickle is oozing, dribbling down my leg as the leech grows fatter and fatter. Oh no. I turn around to Seb, a no doubt horrified expression on my face.

'What?' he asks, or mouths at least. He's too far behind me for me to hear what he's saying.

I point down at my calf. The leech is getting even bigger and the flow of blood trickling down my leg is growing darker and thicker.

'Don't look,' he says from behind me. 'I know we're high up, but looking down will only make it worse.'

He clearly can't see the leech and thinks I'm freaking out about the height of the bridge.

'It's not that, it's my leg. A leech,' I shout back, but Seb frowns incomprehensibly, seemingly unable to hear me.

Oh God. My heart pounds. I can't bring myself to pull off the leech myself. It's too gory and I might faint. I can't turn around to go back to Seb. I'll have to just keep walking, while this leech gets fatter and fatter with my blood.

'Damn it, damn it, damn it,' I spit as I cross the bridge.

I look ahead, accidentally focusing on Helen instead of the trees. She's still taking my picture. Can she not see that I'm in a ton of pain right now?! Now is not the time to take my photo. This is not a funny insta-worthy moment, this is awful. I'm in agony. I feel like crying.

'Helen, will you put the camera down!' I shriek, with such anger and force that I make the bridge shake even more.

Oh God. I grab the handles even tighter, but my palms are so drenched with sweat that I'm starting to feel lightheaded.

My legs are trembling. My whole body is trembling. I cannot collapse on this bridge. I cannot faint up here.

Just keep walking. Ignore Helen. Ignore the leech. Ignore everything. Just get to the other side of this damn bridge.

With renewed drive, I start charging across the bridge, as fast as my feet will carry me. It's rocking, shaking, and bobbing up and down with each step, but I don't care, I just need to get to the other side before this leech demolishes by calf.

'Whoop!' Cody starts cheering as though I'm nearing the finish line of a race. 'Come on, Rachel! You've got this.'

I keep going, ignoring my heart rate, my sweaty palms and the painful stinging.

'Yes, Rachel!' Joe joins in. 'You can do it!'

Helen just keeps taking my picture. The end of the bridge is only five or six metres away. I can make it. Not far. Just a few more steps. I keep walking, steadily, clutching the sides of the bridge until I get to the other side. It's only once my feet cross over onto the land and I collapse onto the ground that I realise Helen, Cody and Joe are clapping, cheering and hollering.

'Are you okay, Rachel? You're white,' Helen says, stooping down next to me.

'No, I'm not!' I groan, still aware of the leech sucking away at my blood. 'Couldn't you see that when you were taking my picture?'

'What?' she replies innocently.

'I'm not okay! There's a leech on my leg,' I tell her.

'Oh man! That's a big one!' Cody comments, his eyes widening at the sight of the giant blood-sucking leech attached to me. I look down at it to see that it's swollen in size, from the size of a skinny worm to a slug an inch wide. My brain starts to go fuzzy.

Seb appears next to me.

'It's okay, Rach,' he says, squatting down next to me and cradling me in his arms.

'Pull it off,' I hear Joe tell Cody, but his voice sounds distant, a bit garbled. I feel like I'm hearing it from the bottom of a well. I'm distantly aware that I'm fainting. The last thing I feel before I lose consciousness is the burning, tearing sensation of a leech being torn from my leg.

When I come around, I look up and see Seb stroking my hair, holding me in his arms. He must have practically sprinted over the bridge.

'Oh, Rachel…' he says softly, his face etched with concern.

'Has the leech gone?' I look down at my leg to see a gaping bloody wound that resembles a cavity adorning my calf.

There's a pile of blood-soaked tissues on the ground that they must have been using to mop up the blood.

My head starts swimming all over again.

'Oh my God,' I utter.

'I'm on it,' Cody insists, although he looks a little white. 'I'm going to patch you up, good as new.'

'Thanks,' I smile gratefully.

'You're like a doctor,' Seb comments to Cody.

Cody laughs. 'You'd be surprised by how many injuries I have to attend to in the gym at work,' he says.

He starts rummaging around in his backpack and pulls out a first aid kit.

Amid my sense of gratitude, I feel a twinge of guilt at how

judgemental I've been towards Cody. He may be a bit annoying with his showy cocky bravado and his cries of "yak attack", but he's also always there in a crisis, knowing what to do, whether that's chew up tree leaves or present a first aid kit, and right now, I couldn't be more grateful to him for his preparedness.

He decants some disinfectant onto a cloth.

'This is going to sting,' he warns.

'Okay,' I reply through gritted teeth, still dazed.

Cody dabs the disinfectant onto my leg and I scream out in agony.

'Oh my God!' I shriek.

The sharp pain cuts through my dazed stupor, waking me up immediately.

'Oh my God that hurts!' I cry.

'Yeah, that leech did a number on you,' Cody says, dabbing on my leg.

'Oh that looks painful!' Helen observes.

I roll my eyes.

'Okay, it's looking better now,' Cody remarks, lifting the bloody gauze off my wound to reveal a slightly less bloody crater.

I feel woozy looking at the sight of it so look at Seb instead. He smiles sweetly at me.

'I'm going to apply some pulp like I did the other day to help your blood coagulate and then bandage you up,' Cody tells me.

'Thanks Cody,' I reply. 'You sound like a doctor.'

Cody laughs.

Seb thanks him too. Joe unzips his backpack and retrieves an energy bar.

'You need to eat,' he says, handing it to me with a sympathetic smile. 'Get your energy levels back up.'

I feel a bit nauseous from the leech, but I know he's right. I take the bar from him and tear it open, taking a bite. Seb hands me a bottle of water. I eat the energy bar as Cody applies a globule of leaf pulp to my wound and bandages up my leg. I have a drink and start to feel a bit better.

'It's done,' Cody says.

I look down at my leg, bandaged up, not a trace of blood in sight.

'Great, thanks Cody,' I reply, feeling genuinely grateful. 'How much blood do you reckon it got out of me?'

'Enough! It was definitely the Dracula of leeches!' Cody says.

The image makes me feel light-headed again.

Seb shoots Cody a look.

'It's gone now. Let's relax here for a bit,' he suggests.

Cody nods. 'Yeah, good plan. Let's just chill here for a while until you get your strength back and then carry on.'

Everyone agrees and settles down for a rest. I still feel woozy and unwell, but I sit up and try to get my strength back.

17 CHAPTER SEVENTEEN

It's getting dark by the time I start to feel normal again and we set off, with two kilometres to go to get to the guesthouse.

'It's not far and there definitely aren't any bridges!' Seb assures me as we walk at a gentle pace along the mountain path.

Helen, Cody and Joe bound along in the distance, having spent the past few hours sunbathing and relaxing. Midges dance in the low light and dragonflies buzz in the shrubbery. I look across the mountains at the setting sun. I glance over at Seb. His skin is glowing, luminous in the golden light. I feel that elephant in the room again. How can we be together twenty-four-seven and go through wild things like suing ashrams and climbing Everest, without talking about the bigger picture? It's not normal, and yet somehow I can't quite bring myself to confront it head-on. What if there's a reason we never talk about our relationship? I know Seb loves me, but not all romances have to last forever, do they? What if he's reasoned that even though what we have is great, it's not for life? Maybe he wanted to come on this trip as one final adventure? One last memory.

The thoughts swirl in my head: fear and doubt clashing with hope, over and over. I have to say something. I have to just get it out there. Broach the subject. It can't be worse than having a leech gorging on your blood and I've been through that already today.

'Seb…' I venture.

'Yeah,' he replies, stepping over a caterpillar that's making its way across the path.

'Umm… Err… What do, umm…' I stammer, not knowing where to start.

What does the future hold? What's next for us?

'What are we, like, doing here?' I ask.

Seb looks at me quizzically. 'Erm, hiking!?' he replies.

I roll my eyes. 'Not hiking! What are we doing? I mean in general. What's this all about?'

Seb frowns. 'Having fun, exploring. What do you mean?'

'Urghh!' I stop in my tracks. A bird squawks in the sky overhead.

'Come on, Seb. You know what I mean. Us. What are we doing? I'm just… Is this our last trip together? What's next?'

'Our last trip?! Of course not,' Seb replies, looking stricken. 'Do you really think that?'

'I don't know! I have no idea. I don't want it to be, but I need to go back to London. I don't know if you're coming. I'm so confused,' I confess.

As I say the words, words that have been pent up inside me for so long, my voice cracks with emotion.

'We'll sort something out,' Seb says. 'I thought we were in this for the long haul?' He looks at me, his expression as uneasy and unnerved as I feel.

'I want to be, of course I want to be. But when we're not talking about it, I start to get worried,' I say. 'I've been going over and over everything in my mind, wondering what the hell is going on.'

'Oh God, Rach, I'm sorry. I thought we were on the same page. I thought we both wanted to stay together. Where there's a will there's a way, right?' Seb says.

I laugh, nodding. That's always been Seb's motto.

'That is true,' I admit.

Seb wraps his arms around me. 'I didn't mean for you to be worrying. I'm sorry.'

He kisses my forehead, seeming genuinely contrite. His reaction is quite surprising. It's as though he's taking personal responsibility for our issues with communication.

'I should have brought it up, I just... I didn't want to spoil the fun. We've already got enough on our plate with this hike!' I comment.

'No.' Seb shakes his head. 'We should have had this conversation earlier. We should really have spoken about all this stuff, but...' he trails off, sighing.

'I felt like I was just trying to go with the flow, live in the moment, you know?' I admit. 'I've done that so much more since I met you and so I was just trying to relax and not overthink everything, but I can't keep it up. I've just been feeling like all these worries about our future have been building inside me, like a weight.'

'Come on, guys!' Cody calls after us.

We carry on walking. I realise, having opened up, just how true my words are. The subject of mine and Seb's future has become a huge weight, a burden I've been carrying for weeks. The court case against Guru Hridaya kept my mind off it for while, but since then, I've been left wondering what the future holds and I've overthought it to the point that I've not known where to begin when it comes to addressing it.

'You shouldn't feel like you have to go with the flow, not when it comes to huge things like relationships,' Seb says. 'Communication is so important. We've always been so open and honest with each other. You know I've never been like this with anyone else before.'

I nod. Seb is my second serious boyfriend, after my ex, Paul. Paul and I started off well. We were like best friends to begin with, and communication between us was always easy and open, but we rapidly grew distant. We both got so busy with work, me especially, and before I knew it, communication between us had broken down. Paul had become really unhappy and unsatisfied in our relationship and yet I was so obsessed with work that I hadn't even noticed. Things had been like that for ages and in the end, we realised that we'd changed and we wanted different things. But with Seb, we've been so close since the first day we met. I'm his first serious girlfriend after a series of flings and short-term relationships and I know he's been making a real effort to make it work. He finds it hard when he feels like he's failing at that.

'Seb, don't worry. We both avoided talking about it. I guess it felt to me like there was too much at stake and for you...' I trail off, realising I'm not entirely sure why Seb didn't want to talk about our future. He seems convinced we're going to stay together so why was he avoiding it?

'I wanted to talk about it,' Seb says. 'I wanted to find the right moment and the right moment just hasn't come about yet, you know? There's been so much drama, from leeches to flirting Canadians to diarrhea, that I just didn't know when to bring it up. And adding hiking Everest into that didn't exactly help!'

'Well, that was your idea!' I point out.

'I know. We'd have probably had a lot more time to chat on a beach holiday,' Seb comments, rolling his eyes.

'Definitely,' I concur.

'Guys! They do beer here!' Cody shouts delightedly.

I've been so immersed in mine and Seb's conversation that I hadn't realised we'd got so close to the guesthouse. Cody is standing outside it in the distance, peering at what looks like a menu on the wall.

Seb laughs. 'See? Never the right moment!'

18 CHAPTER EIGHTEEN

I wake up the next morning, feeling exhausted. A storm raged throughout the night, thunder and lightning crashing across the sky with heavy rain pounding the corrugated roof of my tiny room. Unlike most of the guesthouses we've stayed in so far, our latest didn't have a room for Seb and I to share, so I've spent the night alone, listening to the storm, tossing and turning and trying and failing to sleep despite how tired I felt after the trek. I nodded off for a few hours as the sun was coming up. Groggy, I open my eyes and see that rain has leaked through the roof of my room, trickling down the wall opposite me. I sigh and close my eyes again. Once more an image of my house in London passes through my mind: my lovely bedroom with its nice white wardrobes and dressing table, its sumptuous bed adorned with cushions and throws. What I wouldn't give to be back there now. But no, I'm here, half-way through the Everest Base Camp trek. The thought of trekking today really doesn't appeal. I feel exhausted and the wound on my leg still hurts.

I pull myself into a sitting position. I feel so rough, far rougher than I should be feeling after just a couple of beers last night. Perhaps my alcohol tolerance has gone down, or perhaps I'm just tired. I get up and stretch before heading out of the room and wandering down the hallway to go and see Seb.

I open the door of his room a crack and peer inside, still groggy.

Except it's not Seb I see, it's Cody. And Joe. In bed together, gyrating against each other. Having sex that's so passionate that they don't even notice me.

Joe lets out an orgasmic groan. Oh my God. I back away and close the door instantly. What the hell? I had no idea Joe and Cody were a thing. I had no idea Joe was even gay. I can't believe I just witnessed such an intimate moment. I take another step backwards, still in shock, but the next thing I know, I'm stumbling, staggering back and collapsing onto the floor. I let out a cry of pain as my ankle twists beneath me. A sharp jolt of agony shoots up my leg. I groan.

'Rachel? Rachel? Are you okay?' Joe asks, rushing out of the room.

He's wearing a pair of boxers now, but his skin looks flushed. Even in my pained state, I still feel a bit embarrassed to see him.

'I'm okay, I just twisted my ankle,' I say as I sit back up.

'Ouch. What happened?' Joe asks.

I saw you having sex and was so shocked I stumbled?

'Erm, I just tripped. Must have been a lose floorboard or something,' I lie.

'Ah, I see. You're having a rough time of it, aren't you? Do you want me to go and get you some ice?' Joe asks, looking at me with genuine concern.

'No, it's okay. I'm going to go see Seb,' I say. 'Thanks though, Joe.'

'Anytime,' he replies. 'Well hopefully not anytime. Don't want you twisting your ankle again.'

I laugh. 'I know!'

I get up and hobble to the room on the other side of my bedroom door.

I push it open and fortunately, it is Seb's room. The last thing I need this morning is to walk in on Helen.

'Seb,' I croak, limping towards his bed. He's cocooned in his sleeping bag.

'Yeah,' he grumbles, groggily.

'I just tripped,' I say as I limp towards him. 'Move up.'

Seb's lying on his side, clearly half asleep but he moves up to make space for me. I get into bed with him, pulling the thin guesthouse blanket over myself. My ankle still throbs but I'm so mentally preoccupied by the idea of Cody and Joe that my thoughts are distracting me from the pain.

'Seb, I just saw Cody and Joe, having sex,' I tell him, not sure he's awake enough to take in what I've said.

'What?!' he replies, sounding more alert than I'd expected.

I turn around.

'Yeah, I just saw them having sex.'

'Why were you watching Cody and Joe have sex?!' Seb asks with alarm.

'I wasn't watching them! It wasn't like they gave me a private show!' I scoff.

'Then what do you mean?' Seb asks.

'I just… I went into their bedroom and saw them. I thought it was your room. I just opened the door and there they were,' I tell him.

'Oh no. That's awkward,' Seb replies, sighing.

'They didn't see me. They didn't notice me at all. They don't know,' I explain.

'Oh, right,' Seb says. 'Well, that's something. That would have made for an awkward vibe over breakfast!' He laughs.

'Yeah!' I reply. 'Definitely. Aren't you shocked?!'

'Not really. I knew they were hooking up,' Seb says.

'What!?' I balk.

Since when did Seb know about this?

'Yeah, I didn't want to tell you because… Well, because it's private to Joe really but I knew.'

'What do you mean? How did you know?' I ask, completely

taken aback.

Seb is the kind of guy who people open up to. He's the kind of person that people feel they can trust with their secrets, but even so, I can't believe he's known the whole time.

'The other day when you went to bed early, Joe and I got talking. He seemed really down, kind of stressed and anxious so I asked him what was up. He said he's confused about his sexuality. He said he's always considered himself straight but then he met Cody and they just clicked, and he felt an attraction,' Seb explains. 'He didn't know what to do. He was conflicted on whether to act on his feelings or not. I tried to tell him it was okay and just sort of encouraged him to follow his heart.'

'Well, it worked!' I comment.

Seb laughs.

'I got a bit of an eyeful,' I admit.

Seb raises his eyebrows.

'They definitely didn't see you?' Seb asks.

'Nope. Joe came out a minute later acting completely normal,' I explain.

'Well, that's something. I think he's already self-conscious enough about his sexuality without needing onlookers,' Seb comments.

'Oh my,' I sigh. 'That certainly woke me up.

Seb laughs.

'It's sweet though. So we're not the only ones who are loved-up on this trip then?' I remark.

'Yep. We've lost our status as the loved-up members of the group,' Seb jokes.

I smile. 'Such a shame!'

The birds chirp outside, getting into their morning chorus.

'I'm so surprised though,' I admit. 'I really didn't see that coming. I didn't pick up on any vibes or anything!'

'Neither did I!' Seb says. 'I didn't realise anything had actually happened between them. Maybe they just got together last night after the beers.'

'Maybe! Do you think they'll tell anyone?' I ask.

'I don't know. I think Joe might want to keep it private for a bit,' Seb suggests.

'Yeah, probably.'

A thought occurs to me.

'He was a bit funny the other day when we were all talking about our relationship history, remember? Joe got a bit weird and started blushing. I was wondering what that was about. I guess maybe he was thinking about Cody? Or feeling confused about stuff?' I suggest.

'Yeah, I think so. I noticed that too,' Seb says. 'Anyway, we should probably stop gossiping about them!'

I roll my eyes and give Seb a poke. Unlike myself, Seb tries to avoid any form of gossip.

'Oh, come on! You're not the one who just walked in on them having sex!' I point out.

'True!' Seb laughs. 'Was it really that bad?'

I think back to Joe's orgasmic groan.

'Yes, pretty X-rated!'

Seb pulls a face.

'Anyway! How's the ankle?' he asks.

'Oh yeah!' I reply, having almost forgotten about my twisted ankle.

I'd been so distracted gossiping about Joe and Cody that I'd stopped thinking about the pain. I pull Seb's duvet back and sit up to get a better look. It's swollen and red and looks worse than it feels.

'Ouch!' Seb comments. 'That looks painful!'

'Yeah…' I agree uneasily.

It's not just my ankle that's a state but my calf too, which still bears the plaster Cody stuck on it, which has now crusted around the edges with blood.

I sigh. 'First the diarrhea, then the leeches, now this,' I

grumble.

'You haven't had the easiest time of it since we got to Nepal,' Seb notes.

'No, I haven't,' I admit, my mind wandering to my house back in London once more and how much I wish I was home, in my comfy double bed or having a nice soothing bath. But yet again, I feel guilty for having such thoughts when I should be appreciating the adventure of being in Nepal more.

'We're going to have to rest for a bit,' Seb says. 'You need to heal. You can't trek with your ankle like that.'

I scan Seb's face for signs of frustration or disappointment, but to my surprise, there are none.

'But what about the others?' I ask, thinking of Joe, Cody and Helen.

Seb shrugs. 'They can just go on without us.'

'But…' I think of all the moments we've shared as a group over the past few days – the meals, the photo sessions, crossing perilous bridges, applying sunscreen, tending to leech bites. Even though there are times they've annoyed me, I've sort of got used to them. Is it really all just going to end?

'We've kind of become a group,' I say.

'I know,' Seb replies, 'but we can't really expect them to hang around for us. They'll probably be wanting to be getting on with the trek.'

'I guess,' I murmur, a little surprised. 'Don't you want to be getting on with the trek?' I ask, feeling a little guilty, especially given how much Seb has been wanting to impress his dad.

'Not really,' he says.

He sits up and gently crawls over me, getting out of bed.

'What are doing?' I ask.

'I woke up really early this morning,' Seb says. 'As the sun was rising. I pulled open my curtains and looked out the window. This place is stunning.'

He draws the curtains of his bedroom window open. In the

distance is a lake, its waters bright blue, glowing, like it's been edited in Photoshop. It's surrounded by mountains and looks completely serene and utterly stunning.

'Wow!' I utter, shocked.

By the time we arrived at the guesthouse last night, it was dark. I had no idea the scenery was so spectacular.

'I know!' Seb enthuses.

'It's picture perfect,' I comment.

'Totally. It's beautiful. This whole trekking thing… I'm wondering if it's overrated. When you get that obsessed with reaching your destination, you can start to miss the here and now,' Seb muses. 'If the ashram taught me anything, it was to enjoy the moment.'

I smile. 'I couldn't agree more,' I say, feeling relief washing over me.

'What's so great about physical exhaustion?' I ask. 'It's like we've had to push ourselves to the brink every day to feel some sense of accomplishment. I know Cody loves it. Counting the number of kilometres we've walked, the altitude, the steps, but I don't get it. I can't fully appreciate the scenery when I'm knackered. Or I have leeches gouging chunks out of my leg.'

Seb nods. 'I think Cody was partly trying to impress Joe,' he suggests.

'Oh yeah! Probably!' I laugh, having not considered that before.

I thought Cody was just an annoying show-off, but now I realise he was probably flirting.

'So what shall we do? Just stay here?' I say, a feeling of hope swelling inside.

Seb looks towards the lake and then back to me.

'Yeah, I don't want to go anywhere, and you need to recuperate,' he says.

I smile, relieved.

'Sounds perfect,' I say, letting out a sigh of relief as I lie back down and gaze up at the ceiling of Seb's room. A large insect that looks like a giant ant crawls across the ceiling.

I shudder. 'Maybe we can find a nicer place to stay though,' I suggest. 'These guesthouses only really work when you're completely exhausted.'

Seb laughs. 'We can try, but I doubt they're going to have a five-star hotel around here.'

'I know, but I'd take two stars, three would be amazing. Anywhere without insect infestations basically.'

I point at the ceiling, which the insect is still crawling across.

'Eww!' Seb shudders. 'I probably slept with that thing in here.'

'Well, at least you slept with something!' I joke.

Seb smiles. 'Well maybe I can sleep with something a bit more sexy tonight,' he says, planting a kiss on my lips.

'A bit?!' I reply.

'Yeah, just a bit!' he jokes.

I roll my eyes and kiss him back.

19 CHAPTER NINETEEN

I lie in Seb's bed, my ankle throbbing and sip a cup of coffee Seb fetched me from the kitchen. He's having breakfast with the group and letting them know that we're going to be staying put for a few days. I check my messages. Meera has sent me some more adorable shots of Ajay and Azar, alongside a few selfies. She's looking a little less frazzled and appears to be settling into life as a mum of twins. She sends a few photos of Fred cradling his kids, which are totally adorable. I fire back a string of love heart emojis.

I check to see if Paul has got back to me about the house, but there's nothing. He always promised he'd move out when I was ready to return to London, but what if he's changed his mind? What if he's going to turn it into a big thing and not want to leave? Oh no. I feel a wave of dread wash over me. I send him a text, chasing up, which he probably won't see until the morning since it's the middle of the night back home.

Suddenly, Seb bursts into the room, his face flushed. He shuts the door firmly behind him, his breathing ragged. He seems panicked and totally out of sorts.

'What's happened?' I balk. 'They can't have taken it that badly, surely?!'

'It… it wasn't that, I…' Seb paces the room, frowning.

He doesn't usually stammer or get flustered like this and I can tell something's seriously got to him.

'Fuck,' he spits.

'What is it?' I ask, feeling unnerved. Seb hardly ever gets angry.

He shakes his head, exasperated.

'I went to the kitchen. Helen was there. I told her about your ankle and how we were going to spend a few days here. I expected her to be fine with it, you know. She knows we're together.'

He shoots me a desperate look.

'And?'

'And instead of being okay with it, she came up to me. She was standing really close and saying how she didn't want to do the trek without me. The next thing I know she was touching my arm. She came closer and tried to... kiss me,' Seb spits the words.

'She did what?!'

'I know. She's so deluded. I couldn't believe it.'

I sit up straight, alarmed. 'She tried to kiss you?!'

'Yes.' Seb gulps.

'What did you do?' I ask, wide-eyed with shock.

'I backed away, I told her I was with you. Firmly! I came straight here,' he says.

His voice is quivering and I realise he's shaking a little. He's as upset as I am.

'How dare she?! Who does she think she is? I knew that she was flirting but to actually make a move? That's outrageous.'

'Seb shakes his head. 'I know. She was giving me looks here and there but I didn't think she'd actually make a move!'

'Unbelievable,' I spit. 'She's been flirting with you this whole time. Twerking, giving you looks, wanting you to apply sun cream for her. I've tried to be okay with it but I am not okay with her trying to kiss you.'

'I know,' Seb sighs.

I pull the duvet back and rise to my feet.

'What are you doing?' Seb asks.

'I'm going to say something to her. She can't just go hitting on my boyfriend. She has no respect! I can't believe it!' I bark, fuming.

'Rachel, don't...' Seb says as I start hobbling towards the bedroom door, trying not to put too much pressure on my broken ankle.

'No, Seb,' I snap, holding my hand palm towards him in defiance. 'Don't try to stop me.'

I slip my feet into my flip flops as Seb sighs. I may still be wearing my pyjamas but I don't care.

'It's not worth it,' Seb mumbles.

I roll my eyes.

'Yes, it is,' I insist as I make my way to the bedroom door.

I'd march if I could, I'd stomp towards the door, but thanks to my ankle, my exit from the room isn't particularly dramatic. I can feel Seb watching me disapprovingly.

I head out of the room and scan the corridor for Helen. I hobble towards the kitchen, pumped, wired on adrenalin and anger.

I walk into the kitchen, my head full of all the things I want to say to her, but as I reach it and peer inside, she's not there. Damn. I check a balcony overlooking the lake but she's not there either. She must be in her room.

Sighing, I turn around and hobble back along the corridor towards her room. It's a few doors down from Seb's.

I bang on the door with my fist.

'Helen?' I shout. 'Helen?'

I hear a murmur inside. I can't quite make out what she's saying, but it's definitely her. I decide to just go in. I push the door open, or fling it open. Fling is probably more accurate given the rage that is surging through me.

'What the hell, Helen?' I rage as I hobble into the room, although the sight of Helen sitting on her bed in the corner stops me in my tracks.

She's crying, shaking, clutching her knees to her chest. She looks like a little girl.

'What? What are you crying about?' I ask, puzzled.

Helen looks up. Her face is red and blotchy. The knees of her leggings are damp with tears.

'I'm sorry, I'm just...' Her eyes fill with fresh tears.

I stand in the middle of her room, thrown, not knowing what to do or feel. I'm still angry and yet at the same time, I also feel sorry for her. She looks broken.

'What's going on?' I ask.

She eyes me with a look of fear and hopelessness, before sobbing and lowering her head to her knees.

'I'm sorry,' she croaks, between sobs.

A swell of anger flares up inside me, despite how pathetic Helen looks right now.

'Why did you hit on Seb?' I ask.

'I'm sorry,' Helen repeats.

I roll my eyes, sighing. Her head is still lowered to her knees, like she's refusing to look at me. I begin to feel quite irritated again, in spite of how sad she looks.

'What were you thinking? He's my boyfriend, Helen. Were you just going to try and have an affair with him? Right under my nose?' I spit, realising I'm speaking a lot louder than I meant to. Not shouting exactly, but almost.

'I just... I thought we had a connection,' she says, eyeing me over her knees with a look of shame.

'What? Why? Even if you did, he's with me.' I enunciate the last two words with deliberate emphasis.

'I know,' Helen says.

'I can't believe you did that,' I huff, feeling irritated. I'm tempted to get up and storm, or hobble, out of the room, but Helen looks up at me, her eyes contrite and desperate.

'I shouldn't have. I just... I thought there was maybe something there and I just...' she says in a vulnerable, child-like voice.

'You just what?'

'I just feel so lonely sometimes. I just really want someone,' she says, her eyes filling with fresh tears.

I frown. 'So you thought you'd just take my someone?'

'I know, it was really bad of me. I got carried away in the moment. I'm sorry. I'm just so lonely sometimes. I'm so constantly lonely, all the time,' she says, wiping tears from her eyes, only for fresh tears to appear.

'I'm pathetic, I know,' she continues. 'Do you know what? I came on this trip because I thought I might find someone. How tragic is that? I don't even care about Everest.'

She sobs and I begin to feel my anger abating somewhat. I sit down at the end of her bed.

'I don't care about hiking. I've never been that fussed about travelling, but nothing was working out for me back home. My friends were all meeting guys and falling in love and I was just this fun time girl. Guys never wanted anything serious with me. It was really getting to me so I thought, "I'll go travelling, maybe I'll meet someone different overseas". I came travelling to meet someone. Like a dating quest. I'm so pathetic.'

She looks up at me, but I don't respond, I just stay silent, wanting her to continue.

'Then I met Seb, and I know he's with you and everything, but he's from Montreal, like me. He's so different to the guys I'd been meeting back home. He's so sweet and kind and, like, sensitive. And we have random stuff in common, like how he interned at my dad's company. He's just so nice and cool. I just want someone like that,' Helen explains, looking at me uncomfortably, her face still blotchy.

'So you thought you'd just ignore the fact that he's with me and take my boyfriend? Unbelievable,' I spit, not quite sympathizing with her, even though she does seem completely dejected.

'I'm sorry. I should have known he would never cheat on you.

He adores you. You two are perfect together. And he's too much of a nice guy. I should have known he'd never do anything.'

Helen starts crying all over again, sobbing into her knees.

She looks up, her eyes wet.

'Have you ever just felt, like, so unbearably lonely?' she asks, her eyes lost. She looks like she genuinely wants to know the answer.

I think. I think back to my childhood. It wasn't the easiest time, since my family didn't always have a stable home and we were technically homeless for a few years, but I was never lonely. My parents didn't have much money, but they were loving and caring. I never felt particularly lonely growing up and I always had friends at school. It was the same at university too. I got along with my flatmates and course mates. I felt stressed sometimes with the amount of work I had to do, and I pushed myself hard, determined to do well, but I never felt lonely. And my life after graduation wasn't lonely either. I got together with Paul and spent most of my twenties in a relationship with him. I felt lost and confused for a while after we broke up, but I fell for Seb not long after. So no, I've never really experienced true, overwhelming loneliness. I can't relate to the lost, hopeless look in Helen's eyes. The anger I've been feeling shifts, and I start to feel sympathetic towards her instead.

'No,' I admit, looking down. 'I haven't.'

'Yeah, well it sucks. It really, really sucks,' Helen says. 'I'm not excusing myself but sometimes it's just unbearable. And I guess it makes me do really stupid things. It's why I'm so obsessed with Instagram. I post all these pictures of myself looking happy and carefree and having fun. I always thought I'd fake it until I made it, but I just fake it. I never seem to make it. I get all these likes and people think I'm okay and then I just feel even worse. Even more cut off from the world.'

She sobs again. I still don't feel great about her hitting on Seb, but I can see now that her actions came from a place of true desperation. On the surface, she does look like she has it all. She comes across as beautiful, confident, relaxed, and yet she's secretly so miserable. She's faked being okay so well that she has no support and no one really knows what she's going through.

'It'll be okay, Helen,' I say, reaching over and giving her arm a squeeze.

She looks up at me hopefully. She stops crying and starts drying her face with the edge of her bedsheet.

I think back to how I felt when Paul told me he wanted to break up and go to India to find himself. I was lost back then, similar to how Helen is now. Maybe not quite as bad, but I felt terrible. I couldn't sleep, I was anxious, confused. I felt as if the rug had been pulled out from under me. I booked the first flight out to India to try to win Paul back, rocking up at the ashram in the hope that he'd realise I could be adventurous and free-spirited too and fall back in love with me. Instead, he was horrified that I'd followed him, not letting him have any freedom or space. Looking back on it, it was a bit of a questionable decision, but I wasn't really thinking straight. My judgement was clouded by sadness. Probably similar to how Helen's judgment is a bit off now.

A thought occurs to me.

'Helen,' I venture.

She's spaced-out, staring miserably into the middle distance, but she looks back to me, the focus returning to her eyes.

'Yeah?'

'Why don't you go to the Hridaya ashram?' I suggest. 'I went there when I was feeling really lost and I sort of, found myself there. And I found Seb.'

I may have issues with Guru Hridaya but his ashram is a safe space for lost souls. Most of the Westerners who visit are running from something – a break-up, a break-down, a divorce, a bereavement, all sorts of baggage – and yet they find space at the ashram to relax and heal. There's something about the sunshine, all the rich verdant trees and the birdsong that's so soothing. Not to mention all the delicious vegetarian food, the meditation and yoga classes, the sea not far away. It's the ideal place to take time out when life gets too much. And there are plenty of single people there. Loads of tourists have romances while they're at the ashram. And there's a lot of free love going on too. The night Seb and I first got together, we accidentally stumbled upon an orgy taking place by the ashram swimming pool.

I push the thought out of my mind, the memory still alarmingly vivid.

'It's a really great place. I think you'd really like it. There are loads of friendly people, loads of yoga classes, loads of cool single guys,' I say, with a smile. 'And it's a good place to just unwind. Beats trekking!'

Helen laughs.

'Really? Do you think I should go?'

'Yeah, I really do actually. I think you'd really like it,' I tell her.

Helen smiles. 'I can't believe you're trying to help me,' she says in a small voice.

I laugh. 'Well, I didn't see it coming either. I was livid when Seb told me what had happened, but I get that you're struggling. We all make mistakes.'

Helen smiles.

'Thanks Rachel. Sorry for being such a mess,' Helen comments.

I smile back. 'You really don't come across like a mess. You seem so polished and confident all the time,' I tell her.

Helen laughs, rolling her eyes. 'Glad the act's working then!'

'I guess we all fake it sometimes,' I comment, thinking of how I've been trying to take that I'm easy-going about my future with Seb, even though it's been worrying me every day.

'I really think the ashram would work wonders for you,' I insist.

Helen smiles. 'I think you're right. Going somewhere chilled like that might clear my head. And it would be good to get away from couples. Maybe feeling like the odd one out has started to get to me!'

I laugh. 'So you know about Cody and Joe too then?' I ask.

'Isn't it obvious?!' Helen balks.

'I didn't pick up on it at all!' I remark.

'Seriously? God the tension between them has been simmering for weeks. It started back in Thailand. I could see the chemistry, sparks were flying between them,' Helen says.

'I didn't pick up on anything. It took me walking in on them to realise,' I tell her.

'No way!' Helen says, cupping her hand over her mouth in shock.

'Yep!' I laugh.

We chat away, gossiping about Cody and Joe, and talking about the ashram too – how to get there, what the accommodation's like, how much it costs, the type of classes on offer, all sorts. I even give Helen Meera's phone number so that she has someone to help her get settled in. I'll have to give Meera a heads-up, especially after the whingey texts I've been sending her about Helen. But the truth is, Helen isn't that bad. Now that she's accepted that nothing's going to happen with Seb and apologised, she's actually quite likeable and easy to talk to. She's brightened up a lot, the red blotchiness on her cheeks has faded and she looks her usual self.

'I'd better go back to Seb. He's probably going to think I've murdered you or something!' I joke.

Helen laughs. 'Yeah, you probably should.'

She smiles, a little awkwardly. 'Sorry again Rachel, and thanks.'

I smile back. 'No worries,' I say.

I get up and head back to mine and Seb's room, feeling like a weight has been lifted.

20 CHAPTER TWENTY

When the group hear about my ankle, instead of heading off on the trek without me and Seb, they decide to hang back for a day too. Helen seems a bit exhausted from her emotional outpouring and Joe and Cody are happy to spend a day exploring the lake, without focusing on their step count for once. Maybe they're feeling loved up and want to enjoy each other's company without a gruelling trek getting in the way.

We decide to move to another guesthouse, one without damp stone walls crawling with mysterious insects. Cody goes for a wander and finds a place down the road, which he declares is 'practically like a hotel'. We all excitedly pack our bags and head over there – Cody, Joe and Helen charging ahead with me limping behind with Seb by my side.

The guesthouse turns out to be basic but a lot nicer than the place we'd been staying at before. It's a family home that's been extended to include cosy guestrooms. They're not exactly five star, but Seb and I are given a room with a double bed with crisp white sheets, a big window overlooking the lake and no insects in sight. The view is spectacular and as I drop my bag and sink onto the bed, it's actually quite heavenly.

Helen's laughing at something Joe or Cody said and her laughter carries down the hall.

'I still can't believe you and Helen are getting along!' Seb comments.

He couldn't believe it when I came back from speaking with Helen all relaxed and happy. He'd expected us to have a huge fight. I don't blame him, I'd expected the same.

'I know!' I lie on the comfortable bed, sighing with relief. 'I wouldn't go so far as to say I like her, but I don't dislike her anymore. She's alright. She's just lost.'

Seb sets his bag down by the window, kicks off his shoes and gets onto the bed with me.

'I think it's amazing that you guys made up like that,' he says, reaching out and stroking his fingers along my arm.

'I'm glad too,' I reply.

A bird flies past the window of our room, distracting me. The sunlight shimmers off the water, making it glitter like diamonds. It's so scenic and beautiful and I'm about to comment on the view, when Seb's phone buzzes. We all connected our devices to the WiFi in reception, hoping that this guesthouse has a better connection than the last place. And clearly it does, given Seb's already getting messages coming through.

He pulls his phone from his pocket.

'It's my dad,' he says, pulling a face. 'He's texting saying he wants to chat. I should probably give him a call.'

'Yeah. He's not going to like the fact that we're not hiking,' I comment.

'Screw it!' Seb says, laughing.

He roots around in his bag for his iPad and turns it on. He opens up FaceTime and calls his dad.

'Here goes,' he says as it starts ringing.

'Good luck!' I say, just before his dad picks up.

The screen is dark, Greg's face in shadows.

'Hey Seb!' he says.

'Hey Dad, why's it so dark?' Seb asks.

'I'm in the garage, fixing the car,' Greg says, sounding

strained, not quite in shot as if he's bending at an angle to tend to his repair. 'Give me a second.'

He places his phone down so that Seb and I have a nice view of the ceiling with the sounds of Greg grunting and cursing.

'Had to change a tire. Right, glad that's done,' he says, picking up the phone.

He looks ghoulish in the low light.

'So, how's the trek going?' he says. 'Hi Rachel!' he adds, spotting me.

'Hi Greg!' I reply, waving at the screen.

'We're at Lake Gokyo,' Seb tells his dad.

'Oh, Lake Gokyo, beautiful spot. So, have you not set off for the day yet? What time is it over there?' Greg asks.

Seb looks at the time on the corner of his screen.

'It's 1pm,' he says.

'What?! What are you doing in your room at 1pm? Why are you not hiking?' Greg asks, looking alarmed. 'Are you okay?'

'Yeah, we're good. We've decided to just relax a bit,' Seb says. 'Take it easy for a few days.'

'What?' Greg replies, his face scrunched up in confusion. 'Relax?!' he echoes, sneering.

'Yep!' Seb and I exchange a naughty smile, like deviant children. 'We're just going to enjoy the scenery.'

'Enjoy the scenery?! You go to the beach to enjoy the scenery, not Everest! What are you talking about?' Greg asks, looking genuinely distressed at this point.

I decide to give them a minute to talk this through. For Seb to defy his dad like this is a big deal. I squeeze his knee and give him a sympathetic look, before getting up. Seb smiles at me over the top of his iPad as I pull on my jacket and head out of our room. I close our bedroom door behind me and wander down the corridor towards a balcony, the lake shimmering beyond it. The sight is so mesmerizing that when I step outside, I'm startled to discover Joe and Seb, sitting on a bench. I hadn't seen them from inside.

They're just as shocked to see me and spring apart, with guilty looks on their faces.

I smile at them. 'Guys, I know…' I venture.

I don't mention that I walked in on them having sex. That would be far too embarrassing.

'Oh,' Joe utters, his cheeks turning pink.

Cody puts his arm around Joe's shoulders.

'Sorry Joe, I didn't mean to make you uncomfortable,' I say, feeling awkward at how embarrassed he seems.

'It's cool. I'm just getting used to this side of myself. I never really had an attraction to men before,' Joe admits.

'What can I say?! I'm irresistible,' Cody jokes, grinning.

Joe and I both laugh, the tension dissipating.

Joe makes space for me on the bench and I sit down next to them. We marvel over the view and chat about our plans for the afternoon, agreeing that we should go and get some lunch soon. Helen comes out and joins us and even though things are still a bit weird between us, they're also so much better somehow.

Eventually Seb appears, looking a bit tired and beaten down.

He says hi to everyone and perches on the side of the bench. Seb, Cody and Helen carry on talking about what they feel like having for lunch.

'Are you okay?' I ask Seb in a hushed voice.

'You'd think I'd committed a crime or something,' he groans.

I pull a face. 'Was it that bad?'

'Yeah. Pretty bad, but I think he's coming to terms with it,' Seb comments.

'He'll get over it,' I assure.

'Yeah, hopefully!' Seb jokes.

'I'm proud of you,' I tell him.

He looks at me, a little surprised.

I hesitate before I respond, trying to choose my words carefully.

'Your dad can be a bit…' I'm about to say 'overbearing' when

Seb butts in.

'Of a pain in the arse!' he says.

'Yeah!' I laugh. 'He can be a pain in the arse!' I agree.

Seb laughs. I reach for his hand, lacing my fingers through his. Seb squeezes my hand and we turn our attention back to the group.

They're still discussing lunch.

'I hope they do vegan options,' Helen is saying.

Cody rolls his eyes exaggeratedly. 'Helen, we're half way up Everest!'

Helen shrugs.

Cody shakes his head in disbelief. 'She's going to go and try to find a soya latte, I just know it.'

'Or avocado toast,' Joe comments, snickering.

'Shut up guys!' Helen protests, although despite pretending to be annoyed, she's smiling too.

We get up and head out to lunch.

21 CHAPTER TWENTY-ONE

'Is it just me, or are we in heaven?' I ask Seb as we watch the sun rise over the lake. It's a pale shade of blue that looks so unreal, like nothing I've ever seen before.

'Pinch me,' Seb jokes. 'We're dreaming.'

I pinch him. 'Ouch!' he replies and pinches me back.

'Okay!' I yelp. 'We're definitely not dreaming!'

Seb grins.

The sun rises higher into the sky. I lie, in Seb's arms, feeling totally blissed out, not just from the view. We made the most of having a double bed after so many nights of having to sleep separately in twin beds.

'I don't want to ever leave this place,' I gush.

'You don't mean that, I know you miss London,' Seb comments.

'Yeah, I know, but this is just so stunning. I'm never going to forget this,' I remark, turning to Seb.

I feel a swelling sensation in my heart. The love I have for him is so intense. Ever since we met, life has been so much better. We've done things together that I would never have dreamed about back home. He's taught me to appreciate nature and adventure in a way I never really did before. He's opened up the world to me. And yet he's right, I do miss London. I miss little things, like Marks & Spencer ready meals. I miss getting a coffee in the morning from Costa. I miss the hustle and bustle of London during my lunchbreak at work, feeding the pigeons scraps of sandwiches while chatting to Priya in the courtyard outside the office like we've done for years. I miss getting dressed up and wearing nice suits and coats and sharp outfits, rather than just t-shirts and shorts or the hippyish hareem pants I've worn for months on end. I miss wearing smart shoes instead of flip-flops and godawful hiking boots. I miss my house and having my own personal space and all my things around me. Even though being on an adventure has been fun and I've made memories during this trip that I'll never forget, I've also missed feeling of being home.

'You know, I've been thinking about the future,' Seb says.

My heart lurches. Is this it? Is this the moment when we discuss us? Our lifelong plans? Seb looks a bit nervous. Is he as tense about this as I am?

'I've been thinking about what I'm going to do for work,' Seb says.

'Oh,' I reply, surprised, my heart sinking a little bit, before curiosity replaces my disappointment. 'What are you thinking?

'I've kind of had this idea for a while, but I guess I was just all wrapped up in trying to prove a point. I felt like I should go back into international relations, get a corporate job,' Seb says glumly.

I smirk.

'What!?' he replies. 'Why are you looking at me like that?'

'Sorry, you're just not corporate!' I say, cuddling up to him.

'I know!' he laughs. 'I know I'm not, but I sort of felt like I should be. I think I've had this chip on my shoulder, like I need to prove a point to my dad. And then yesterday, when I told him we weren't hiking, I just realised I don't need to live my life according to his standards.'

Seb pauses, frowning.

'I'm nothing like him, but sometimes I feel like I just want him to be proud of me so I try to please him. It's so pathetic, but he's my dad, you know? But the thing is, he's never happy with anything I do and I think I need to accept that and just focus on making myself happy instead,' Seb says.

I smile sadly. I feel for him. His dad is always criticizing him, not just his approach to hiking but him being in India, his love of spirituality and meditation, his passion for yoga, his interest in mindfulness. His dad pushes him on the job front too, always asking him what his 'long-term plan' is. I get that maybe he's concerned about Seb's prospects and I've tried to write it off as tough love but constantly putting pressure on Seb isn't helping him grow, it's just been making him miserable. It's been making him stressed and inhibiting his confidence and ability to thrive, rather than supporting it.

'Your dad's a completely different person to you,' I comment. 'I think he needs to give you more space to do your own thing.'

'I know. That's it. I'm going to do my own thing,' Seb says, nodding to himself, a look of determination in his eyes.

'What are you going to do?' I ask.

'Well, you know how into fitness I am,' Seb says.

I nod.

'I was thinking of doing something around fitness, but I realised I wanted to bring in meditation and yoga and mindfulness into it too. I thought I could do personal training, but take a kind of holistic and spiritual approach to it, focusing on the mind and the body. I can draw on my experiences at the ashram of getting physically fit and becoming happier and enlightened mentally,' Seb explains.

I can tell from his nervous and slightly wide-eyed expression that this is probably the first time he's told anyone about this idea and yet I get the impression he's been thinking about it for a while. It clearly means a lot to him. I think about how much Londoners would love holistic personal training. They'd lap up the idea of being taught by someone who went on their own spiritual journey in an ashram.

'I think that's a brilliant idea, Seb. It's perfect for you,' I tell him, meaning it.

Seb is a natural people-person. He's effortlessly charming. Everyone always seems to warm to him, whatever their age or background. He just has a way with people. Personal training, being so face-to-face, would be perfect for him. And it's not corporate at all.

'Do you really think so?' Seb asks, his face lighting up.

'Definitely. It's such a good idea. It couldn't be more perfect for you,' I tell him. 'You wouldn't be sitting behind a desk. You'd get to help people. I think it's a brilliant idea.'

Seb smiles and lets out a sigh of relief.

'I'm so glad you like the idea too.'

'You could be like Jay Shetty and write a book about fitness but with mindfulness tips too,' I suggest.

Seb raises an eyebrow, seemingly unaware of the multi-millionaire motivational Instagram influencer who lived as a monk in Mumbai before trying to make wisdom go viral.

'You know how his thing is how he used to be a monk, yours can be how you used to live in an ashram. People would love it. Fitness the spiritual way,' I say. 'Might need to work on that slogan a bit.'

'Needs more alliteration,' Seb agrees.

I think for a moment. 'Fulfilment through fitness? Spiritual... sprints?' I suggest, grimacing.

Seb winces. 'Yeah, we need to work on that slogan!'

'Yeah, I think you might be right,' I admit. 'I think it's a great idea though. I'm so happy that you've stopped trying to please your dad. You're not him and he needs to get over that. You need to do you. You're amazing,' I say, feeling a bit slushy. I know I sound sentimental, but I don't care. It's true.

Seb smiles. 'Thanks Rach,' he says.

We lie in each other's arms for a while longer as the sun soars over the mountains. I'm about to broach the subject of our long-term plans and how we're going to make things work, but I can't quite bring myself to. The sunrise is so spectacular and yet I can't decide if now is the perfect moment to confirm our long-term future together or if I'll ruin it by having an awkward conversation. Essentially, in bringing up our long-term future, I'm asking Seb if we're going to get married since it would be the only way we could get visas to stay together. Back when I lived my life according to a Life List, I'd wanted to get engaged by thirty and as I approached my 31st birthday, I was so desperate to tick off my goal that I'd lost sight over whether myself and my boyfriend, Paul, were actually compatible anymore. When our relationship fell apart, I realised that obsessing over my Life List had not been improving my life, but had instead been working against me. In the end, I abandoned the idea of my Life List entirely and just started going with the flow, and even though I've embraced that approach and I'm a lot more relaxed about things than I used to be, I can't deny that I do still want to get married. It does mean something to me and there's still a raw, slightly bruised side of me that's been rejected once before at a time when I thought marriage was on the cards, and I don't want to feel that pain again.

'I think I might go for a run,' Seb says, interrupting my thoughts.

'Oh, okay,' I reply.

'Speaking of being a fitness guru...' Seb jokes.

'Yep. Got to practice what you preach!'

'Exactly!' Seb smiles, getting up from the bed.

He puts on his shorts, T-shirt and trainers and heads out.

I grab my phone from the bedside table and decide to catch up with people back home. I open my messages to see that Paul has been in touch. Paul! Finally. I feel a hint of nervousness as I open his message. He's been avoiding me for weeks and I've started to get worried about what the reason behind it could be.

Paul: Hi Rachel, sorry I've not been in touch. Been really busy with work. I'm in relationship now with a girl I used to go to school with - Suzie. She got a job down in London and we got talking over Facebook. We're moving back up north at the end of the month. We've both got new jobs there and I think it will suit us better than London, and we'll get to be near family. I won't be needing to stay in the house, it's all yours. We can figure out the finances later. Hope you are having a great trip. Paul.

I feel a wave of relief as I read the message. It's a bit annoying that he's been delaying messaging me just because of work, but still! He's moving out and the house is all mine! Seb and I can move in and start a life together! I also find that despite everything that Paul and I went through, I feel happy for him. I'm glad he's found someone who seems to want the same things he wants. Despite trying to get involved in London life as much as he could, Paul never really let go of his roots. From watching every Manchester United match to whinging about London prices and comparing them to prices up north, he never really let home go.
     I write a reply.

Me: Hey Paul, good to hear from you. Good news about your new relationship – I'm happy for you. Also, happy to hear about the house!

I add some details about confirming his move-out date and we message back and forth for a bit, discussing practicalities like the handover of keys and settling outstanding bills. It's all perfectly amicable and I feel myself getting excited as we message. Soon I'll be back home in my lovely little house. Hopefully with Seb by my side and a happy future ahead of us.
     Having sorted things out with Paul, I catch up with a few other friends. I post a picture of the view from the window on Facebook

with a string of love heart emojis and then message Priya. It's 7.30am here so it will be around 2pm over in London. If I'm lucky, I might catch her on her lunchbreak. I send her a message and she fires one back instantly.

Priya: Hey girl! How's Everest?!

I message her a picture of the view and tell her that Seb and I have taken a break from the trek because of my ankle.

Priya: WOW! Beautiful. Are you ok?

Me: Yeah, I'm fine. My ankle will be fine. Just a bit confused about a few things. You're not free to chat, are you?

Priya calls back a moment later. I pick up the phone, feeling so happy to speak to her. It's been weeks.

'Hey!' I say excitedly as I answer.

'Hey! Oh my God, stranger! How are you?' Priya replies, sounding as excited as I feel.

It feels so good to hear her voice again.

'Well, Everest has been quite the experience,' I tell her, launching into the full story of Helen, Cody and Joe, as well as the perilous bridges, grim guesthouses and leeches.

'Leeches?!' Priya balks.

'I know!' I sigh. 'I've still got a bandage on my leg from the last one sucking the blood from my calf. It left this massive cavity, it was-'

'Stop!' Priya protests. 'I'm eating! That is rank!'

I laugh. 'Oh sorry!'

I ask Priya about work and she gives me the lowdown on office life and tells me how Rene's business is going, telling me how he just secured start-up funding for his latest business venture.

'That's amazing. Tell him congrats from me!' I say.

'I will. How's Seb?' Priya asks.

I tell her about Seb's new career plan and how I reckon he could be the Jay Shetty of personal training.

'I love that!' Priya laughs. 'So he's coming to London then?'

I gulp. That's the big question. I need to get my worries off my chest.

'Well, he seems to want to stay together. He's made it clear that's what he wants, but we haven't talked about the logistics yet. We haven't gone into exactly how that would work, you know?'

'You mean visa-wise?' Priya says.

'Exactly. If Seb's going to stay in London, the easiest way to guarantee he gets a visa is if we get married! He seems to see us staying together so I think he might want to. I don't know,' I say, sounding more vulnerable than I realised I felt.

'Wow! Marriage!' Priya gushes. 'This is huge.'

'I know!' I reply. 'But I love him. We're so good together. I'd love to be married to him.' My voice cracks up and I gulp.

Maybe you should... ask him?' Priya ventures.

I hear the sound of London traffic in the background, a car horn.

'Ask him to marry me?' I say.

'Well, yeah, or address the issues,' Priya says.

'I know, we need to talk about it. I guess I do want to ask him, I just don't want to do it in a really clinical way, like "should we get married so you can get a visa?". It sounds so transactional,' I explain.

'So, why don't you ask him for real?' Priya suggests. 'Do a proper proposal.'

I nod, even though Priya can't see it. It feels good to have her confirm the idea that's been building in the back of my mind.

'I think that's what I'm going to do,' I say.

'Really?' Priya asks excitedly.

'Yeah! I think I will!' I reply, my trepidation morphing into excitement.

'I love this! Oh my God! How are you going to do it? When?' Priya asks.

'I don't know! I've only just decided to go for it, give me a minute!'

Priya laughs.

I hear footsteps along the corridor outside.

'I think Seb's coming back from his run. I'd better go,' I say.

'Okay, keep me posted!' Priya insists.

'I will!' I tell her.

I say goodbye and hang up as Seb comes into the room, sweaty and out of breath and totally oblivious to the fact that I'm about to pop the question.

22 CHAPTER TWENTY-TWO

Unsurprisingly, it's not exactly easy to buy an engagement ring up Everest. I told Seb I wanted to go for a walk to 'clear my head' and began scouring the area, hoping I might be able to find something that resembled a ring for sale. There are a few guest houses near the lake and a couple of small restaurants. There's one tiny shop selling postcards and souvenirs, but it didn't have any rings. They're not exactly top priority when you're hiking, but I'd hoped that it might have something. Loads of the tourist shops back in the cities sell jewellery and clothes aimed at tourists and I was hoping I might be able to buy a cheap ring. It wouldn't be anything fancy, but it would serve the purpose of my proposal. But there was nothing.

Sighing, I slump down on a wall, wondering what to do. I gaze at a nearby tree, my eyes roaming over its branches. Maybe I could make something? I reach for a branch and inspect the thickness and pliability of its offshoots. Could I fashion a ring out of it?

'Erm, why are you fondling that tree?' Joe asks, appearing next to me.

'Oh, hey!' I say, letting go of the branch.

Joe regards me with a curious expression.

'Hey,' he says, sitting down next to me. 'What's up?'

I sigh and look over at him, wondering if I should open up. He looks back at me, his eyes wide and welcoming. I decide to trust him. Afterall, he's made himself pretty vulnerable in the past few days.

'I want to propose to Seb,' I admit. 'But I need a ring!'

Joe's face lights up. 'Oh my God! That's such great news! You guys are perfect for each other!'

He grins, pulling me into a hug. He seems genuinely delighted for me and I find myself grinning back.

'I'm so happy for you!' Joe enthuses. 'What made you decide to go for it now?'

'Well, I love him. I've never been in love like this before,' I tell him.

Joe smiles, a sweet, wistful expression on his face. His eyes look a little teary, like he's genuinely moved. He really is a sensitive soul.

'And we need to get married if we're going to make this work long-term, for visa reasons. But it's not about that. I'd marry Seb anyway, in a heartbeat,' I admit, tears springing to my eyes now too.

'Aww!' Joe pulls me into another hug and we both flick tears away.

'So when are you going to do it?' he asks.

'As soon as I can really,' I say. 'I just need a ring. I've been looking around for one, but unsurprisingly, there aren't many for sale up here.' I sigh. 'That's why I was fondling the tree. I was thinking maybe I could make a ring out of it.'

Joe looks over my shoulder and raises an eyebrow at the tree behind me. 'Really?!'

I shrug. 'Do you have any better ideas?'

'Yeah! Have you not met Soneeya?' he says.

'Who?'

'Soneeya. She's a local craftsperson. She sells jewellery and dream catchers and all sorts. Cody and I got chatting to her last night. He got a load of stuff for his mum. She lives around the corner,' Joe says.

I laugh. 'I can't believe you know a local ring seller!'

Joe grins. 'You know me, I like to get to know the locals,' Joe says.

'Yeah, I know you do,' I reply, smiling.

I realise just how wrong I got Joe and Cody when I first met them. I thought they were these annoying alpha guys but there's so much more to them. Joe is so sweet and kind-hearted, and even though Cody is a on the louder, cockier side, he's a great guy too. He's always there for you in an emergency and he's the kind of guy who buys a load of jewellery for his mum up Everest, carrying it around the world for her. I thought I'd developed as a person in India, becoming a better version of myself, but I now realise that I still had a long way to go. India took me out of my comfort zone and led me to develop gratitude and an ability to relax and go with the flow a bit more, but Nepal has helped me to become less judgemental about other people. It's helped me realise that there's so much more to people than meets the eye.

'So, do you want to meet Soneeya?' Joe says.

'Do I ever!' I reply.

Joe grins as we hop off the wall and head off to Soneeya's house. Joe explains how he and Cody went for a walk last night and found her sitting in her front garden, selling her wares to a group of hikers.

'I think she does a pretty good trade,' Joe comments.

'I'm so excited to meet her.'

We arrive outside a ramshackle little house tucked into the mountain. A stream trickling alongside a front garden blooming with exotic flowers.

Joe taps on the front door.

There's no response.

'Maybe she's out,' I say. 'Or maybe she just doesn't want to be disturbed.'

Joe pulls a face. 'Yeah, maybe.'

We wait a few moments longer before sighing and turning to leave, when suddenly the door opens to reveal a small elderly lady standing in the doorway with a quizzical expression on her face that quickly transforms into a smile when she recognises Joe.

'Hello Joe!' she says. 'How are you? Come in.'

'Namaste,' she adds to me as she beckons us into her home.

'Namaste,' Joe replies, bowing gently in respect.

'Namaste,' I add.

'Sorry to disturb you, Soneeya, I was just telling my friend, Rachel, about your beautiful jewellery.'

'No problem. You are welcome.'

Soneeya leads us into her front room, which has an indoor outdoor feel, being full of pot plants and flowers. There's a small settee and an armchair and a work bench covered in metal, tools and beads.

'You want to see my jewellery?' Soneeya asks, looking at me.

'Definitely!' I enthuse. 'I'd love to.'

'Okay, I'll show you. You want tea?' she asks me and Joe.

'Oh yes, please, you don't have to though,' Joe says.

'No problem. Please, sit,' Soneeya says.

We sit down and admire the room. Soneeya comes back with a silver pot of tea and cups. She sets it down on the coffee table before us and pours the steaming tea into cups. It's mint tea and smells deliciously fresh. She asks me questions about where I'm from and tells us a bit about her life, growing up in the north India village of Orccha before moving here with her late husband who was Nepalese and worked as a tour guide.

'It's a beautiful place,' I comment. 'I felt like I was in heaven waking up here this morning.'

She smiles. 'I feel that way too.'

She sets her cup down and walks over to her workbench. She reaches for a box and brings it over, placing it down on the coffee table, before opening it to reveal a colourful array of bangles and necklaces, beaded and shimmering. They're beautiful. I reach for a red beaded necklace with an engraved pendant. The beads are the brightest shade, shiny and intricate, and the pendant is bold and striking, with a unique design like nothing I've ever seen for sale back home.

'Wow, this is stunning!' I comment, admiring it.

'Oh yeah, I like that one too. Do you want to try it on?'

'Sure,' I reply.

Soneeya hands me a mirror. I drape the necklace around my neck and admire my reflection. I don't usually tend to wear red. It washes me out a bit. I usually go for blues and greens, colours that match my eyes.

'That looks beautiful,' Soneeya gushes and even though I don't usually wear red, I have to admit, I agree.

The necklace is such a striking design that I look almost regal. Although I know the design would suit Priya better and would make a brilliant gift for her. I take it off and ask how much it costs.

'Nineteen hundred rupees,' Soneeya replies, which is about £12. Possibly quite a lot in Nepal but definitely worth it.

I spot another necklace in the box, this one comprised of coral pink beads that my mum would just love.

'Oh wow! This is gorgeous,' I comment, reaching for it.

'What about the ring?' Joe reminds me.

'Oh, yeah, in a minute,' I reply.

Once I've got a necklace for Priya, Meera, my mum, my other two best friends from back home - Sasha and Julia, and even a bracelet for my dad, I finally turn my attention to rings.

Soneeya takes another box from her work bench and presents it to me. It contains handmade rings in silver and bronze with natural stones inset. The rings have an artisan handmade feel and they're not like the type of polished sparkling engagement rings you could pick up in Hatten Garden back home, and yet I can't imagine Seb wanting a ring like that anyway. He'd prefer something with a handmade feel and a story to it. I root around in the box and find a battered bronze ring with a tiny blue stone. The shade of blue reminds me of Seb's eyes. It reminds me of the azure blue skies we've seen over the mountains and of the striking blue of the lake this morning. It feels right.

'I'd love this one,' I say.

I ask Joe to try it on since his hands look similar to Seb's. It's too small for him so Soneeya takes it, places it on a ring mandrel and begins hammering away at it with a mallet to stretch it. Once she's got it big enough to comfortably fit on Joe's ring finger, she hands the ring to me. I hold it between my fingers, admiring it in the light pouring through the window. The blue stone twinkles in the light.

It's perfect.

23 CHAPTER TWENTY-THREE

Engagement ring in my pocket, I walk towards the shimmering lake.

Joe has gone back to the guesthouse to hang out with Cody. I should probably be heading back soon too, but the lake looks so beautiful that I can't resist exploring. A Nepalese man standing next to a small flotilla of rowing boats is talking to a few tourists. I linger nearby and overhear that the tourists are asking to a rowing boat out on the lake. Like us, they must have decided to take a break from hiking. The man negotiates a price with them.

I have an idea. I could do it here! I could propose to Seb on one of these little rowing boats in the middle of the lake. It would be so romantic.

I ask the man if it would be possible to take a boat out for an hour. He agrees. I thank him and get my phone out to message Seb, my heart fluttering in my chest. I'm really doing this! I'm asking Seb to marry me.

Me: Hey, can you meet me at the lake? X

He replies almost instantly.

Seb: OK! Be there in five x

I sit on a bench and look out at the view: bright sparkling water, flanked by soaring mountains, the sky clear and endless. The tourists row out into the lake and I watch their boat retreat. I feel nervous and excited, but mostly nervous. To think, not so long ago, I was walking into a restaurant in London to meet my ex, feeling convinced he was going to propose to me. Instead, he broke up with me and I realised he wasn't the one for me anyway. Never in a million years did I think I'd end up sitting by a lake in Nepal, ready to propose to a guy I met in an ashram in India! Sunlight shimmers off the lake. I don't think I could have found a more perfect place to propose. I just have to hope Seb says yes.

I hear footsteps behind me and turn around.

'Hey you,' Seb says as he approaches.

'Hey!' I reply.

He comes and sits next to me on the bench.

'You okay?' he asks, frowning at me slightly. He must be able to pick up on my nerves.

'Oh yeah, I'm good. I thought we could take a boat out?' I suggest, gesturing towards the man and the rowing boats.

'That sounds fun,' Seb replies.

'Excellent!'

We head over to the boats and pay the man to take one out.

We clamber into the boat, treading gently as it moves on the water.

'Do you want to row or shall I?' Seb asks.

'Can you?' I suggest, figuring that proposing while rowing might be a bit complicated.

'Sure,' Seb says, sitting down and taking hold of the oars.

I sit opposite him at the end of the boat as he begins to row into the lake.

'So what have you been up to? How was your coffee?' he asks.

'Oh, it was great!' I reply, smiling awkwardly, not wanting to admit that actually I ran into Joe and I've been buying an engagement ring.

'What have you been doing?' I ask.

'Oh, I was just reading on the balcony,' Seb tells me.

Seb rows further from the bank. I reach down to the water, touching it with my fingertips, causing its surface to ripple. The water is icy cold and the most unreal shade of blue.

'This is such a beautiful spot,' Seb comments.

He stops rowing for a moment and takes his camera from him pocket. He points it at me and I smile, while he takes a few pictures.

'Shall I do a Helen?' I joke. 'Take seventy-five pics and choose the best.'

Seb laughs. 'I already got a beautiful shot,' he says.

I consider asking to take a picture of Seb, but I feel on edge – excited and nervous. I can't think of anything, but the proposal and I'd rather take a shot of us once we're, hopefully, engaged.

Seb takes a few pictures of the scenery.

While he's distracted, I take the ring from my pocket and enfold it in my palm.

'Seb...' I venture, my heart thumping in my chest.

I'm really doing this. I'm proposing!

I wait for him to put the camera down.

'There's something I want to ask you,' I say.

'What's that?' he asks, frowning slightly.

'Umm... Well, you know how much I love you, don't you?' I say.

'Yeah, I know,' Seb replies, smiling sweetly.

'I don't think I've ever met anyone more perfect for me then you. I feel lucky every day that I found you. You're just everything to me. You make me smile, you inspire me, you make me feel like a better person. Every day with you is an adventure. I love being around you I can't imagine my life without you,' I tell him.

Seb smiles, his expression both bemused and sincere.

'I feel the same,' he says. 'I adore you.'

'I know you do. I love being with you. I know we're from different parts of the world and we haven't been together for that long, but I couldn't be more sure of how much I love you. I truly don't think I could ever love anyone like I love you.'

Seb's eyes widen and I think it dawns on him where this is heading.

I open my hand to reveal the ring. I hold it between my fingers as Seb eyes it, with both surprise and delight.

'What I'm trying to say is, I want to spend the rest of my life with you, Seb,' I tell him, gazing into his eyes, which are full of tenderness.

'Seb, will you marry me?' I ask, presenting the ring to him.

'Yes!' Seb replies.

His eyes fill with tears of joy.

'I can't believe it!' he exclaims as I place the ring on his ring finger.

'It fits!' I enthuse, delighted.

We kiss and Seb holds me in his arms. My heart swells with happiness. I feel like the luckiest person alive. The love of my life has agreed to marry me. All of the fears and worries I've been carrying around for weeks dissipate. We're going to be together.

'I can't believe you asked,' Seb comments once we finally pull apart.

'I had to. I don't want to be apart from you. The idea of losing you is unbearable. I want to be with you forever,' I tell him. '

Seb smiles.

'I wasn't sure if you'd say yes. I know you love me, but we've only been together for six months. I just knew I wanted to be with you and this way, we can. Nothing can stop us. And it feels right,' I say.

Seb nods. 'It does. You beat me to it,' he comments.

'Huh?'

'You beat me to it!' He reaches into the pocket of his jeans and pulls out his wallet.

He opens it and fishes a ring out of one of the pockets. It's a beautiful platinum band with a diamond. I gasp, clapping my hand over my mouth.

'I've been carrying this around for weeks! I was going to ask you to marry me on the last day of our base camp trek. I thought it would be romantic, to propose to you on Everest!' Seb tells me.

'No way!' I utter.

'Yes. That's why when you started asking me about our plans for the future the other day, I was being a bit vague. I started feeling bad. I felt like I was avoiding the topic a bit, but the reason was because I wanted my proposal to be a surprise. I want to marry you. I don't care where we live, I just want to be with you,' Seb tells me.

I laugh, unable to believe it.

'I was beginning to worry. I had no idea you wanted to propose!' I admit.

'Of course, I did. You know how much I love you,' Seb says. 'I can't believe you beat me to it!'

I laugh.

'Sorry about that. You can still propose if you want!' I suggest.

Seb grins.

'Okay!'

He moves the oars aside and kneels in front of me.

'Rachel, I love you. You're my soulmate. Ever since you walked into the ashram, I've been drawn to you. Like a magnet, I've just felt this urge to be around you. I've never been so comfortable or in tune with anyone. We're so in tune with each other that even our proposals clashed!' Seb says.

I laugh, rolling my eyes.

'Rachel, will you marry me?' Seb asks.

I grin, delighted.

'Of course, I will!'

Seb places the ring onto my ring finger. It's beautiful – a stunning, elegant ring that's far more traditional than the one I've given him.

'I can't believe this!' I gush, admiring the ring, which twinkles in the sunlight. 'It's such a beautiful ring, Seb!'

Seb smiles. 'I'm so glad you like it.'

'When did you get it? Where?' I ask.

'I bought it in Mumbai,' he says. 'When I had that business meeting.'

I think back to the conference Seb had in Mumbai. It was six weeks ago!

'You've been planning this for six weeks?' I balk.

'Yep!' Seb admits. 'I knew I was going to propose but I just wanted to find the right moment. Then when we decided to go to Nepal, I figured Everest would be ideal, but you beat me to it!' Seb laughs.

I shake my head, laughing too, unable to believe the crazy coincidence.

'It's a beautiful ring, Seb,' I comment, holding my hand out to admire it as it twinkles in the sunlight.

I know Seb tends not to care about jewellery or fancy clothes, but he's gone all out with the ring to try to make me happy. He knows my taste and that I like traditional good quality things and he's bought me something truly beautiful. No wonder he was doing so much translation work.

'Thank you, Seb,' I say, truly meaning it.

'Anything for you, Rachel,' he replies.

He comes over and sits with me at the end of the boat. I lie back and sink into his arms. I lace my left hand through his, our engagement rings side by side. The boat ebbs gently on the water, the mountains soar towards the sky and the sun shines brightly. A bird flaps its wings, soaring across the horizon.

'I can't wait to spend the rest of my life with you,' I say.

'Me neither,' Seb replies, leaning in to kiss me.

22 CHAPTER TWENTY-FOUR

Two Months Later

I always thought I'd have a white wedding. I pictured a quaint little church in a pretty village. I imagined an aisle full of flowers and rows of smiling guests. I thought I'd have a big flowing white gown with a veil. I imagined a priest, confetti, a photographer, the works. What I didn't imagine was a tiny rundown registry office in southeast London on a grey Tuesday afternoon and yet as Seb and I walk inside, hand in hand, I can't stop smiling.

I'm not wearing a big white dress. I'm wearing a cool copper-coloured silk slip I found in a little boutique in Covent Garden. And I don't have a veil. Instead, I've got a headband on adorned with little silk roses. I don't have a load of bridesmaids by my side, but I have Priya, and she can't stop smiling either. And I have Meera! Meera and Fred flew all the way from India to share our special day and I got the chance to meet my godchildren, the little Ajay and Azar, who are absolutely adorable. Meera may have had her concerns about being a mum to twins, but she's completely smitten with her boys. It feels amazing to have her and her family by mine and Seb's side, knowing how if it wasn't for meeting at her guesthouse and for her playing Cupid at the start of our relationship, we might not even be together.

Seb and I aren't walking into a little country church packed full of our friends and relatives. Instead, we just have my mum and dad with us and Seb's dad, Greg. Yes, Seb's dad! He came all the way from Canada for our wedding. He and Seb had a massive heart-to-heart and he apologized for all the pressure he'd been putting on Seb to trek up Everest, get a corporate job, live his life in a certain way. He admitted that he'd been projecting himself onto Seb and in his own weird way, thinking that he was somehow helping Seb live up to his potential. Or what he thought was his potential, but was actually a reflection of his own frustrated hopes and dreams. He agreed he'd taken it too far though and had started becoming quite toxic and harsh. He and Seb had a big heart-to-heart and now they're getting along fine. Greg's even clicked with my dad. I didn't think they'd have anything in common, but it turns out they have a few shared interests, like an appetite for books on military history and both o them enjoy fishing, and even as we enter the registry office, they're chatting and laughing.

We walk into the registry office and a receptionist directs us to the chapel room where we're going to take our vows. It resembles a conference room, but has a few touches to make it feel a bit like a wedding venue, with a few vases of flowers and flickering candles. There are around thirty chairs inside, facing a desk where the registrar sits, waiting for us. My heart is beating hard and fast in my chest and my palms are beading with sweat. We're doing this!

Our guests sit down and Seb and I stand before the registrar, who rises to her feet. Seb and I hold hands, smiling, gazing into each other's eyes.

'Ready?' The registrar asks.

'Ready!' I reply.

The clerk laughs. 'You two do look it!'

She opens a book and launches into the vows.

'Today Seb and Rachel will declare their love and commitment to one another and publicly affirm their marriage...'

As the registrar continues, it hits me just how far Seb and I have come. From meeting in an ashram guesthouse to standing in a registry office, committing to be together for life.

'For Seb and Rachel, getting married here today is a confirmation of the love, respect and friendship that they have for each other,' the registrar says, smiling sweetly at us. 'Together they have found happiness and fulfilment and it is in this spirit that they have chosen to affirm their relationship with this formal and public pledge.'

I'm aware of our guests smiling, happy for us, but it feels like the world has just shrunk to me and Seb. It feels like my whole life has led me to this moment. I've finally found the one. My other half. And we're going to be together forever. My heart thumps in my chest and my hairs stand on end as the clerk reaches the most important part of the ceremony.

'Seb, if you repeat after me. I Sebastian John Auclair,'
Holding my hands, Seb looks into my eyes.
'I, Sebastian John Auclair,' Seb repeats.
'Take thee, Rachel Watson,' the registrar says.
'Take thee, Rachel Watson,' Seb repeats.
'To be my wedded wife.'
'To be my wedded wife.'
'To love and to cherish.'
'To love and to cherish,
'For the rest of my life.
'For the rest of my life.'

I smile, feeling like the luckiest woman alive. Then it's my turn.

I try to hold it together as I make my pledges to Seb, even though I feel choked up and emotionally overwhelmed. I make it through and the registrar affirms the importance of marriage and the commitment we're making.

'Seb, do you promise to love, cherish and care for Rachel for the rest of your lives together?' she asks Seb.

'I do,' he says, smiling sweetly.

'And Rachel, do you promise to love, cherish and care for Seb for the rest of your lives together?' she asks.

'I do,' I say.

We move on to the exchange of rings. It's an effort to hold it together as Seb slides my wedding ring onto my finger, vowing that I will 'be in his heart always'. I promise that Seb will 'be in my heart always' and 'I will be true to him until the end of my days' and slide his wedding ring onto his ring finger.

I glance at Priya who flicks a tear from her eye.

People say that when you die, your life flashes before your eyes, but I feel almost like that now. It feels like everything I've been through, my childhood dreams of wanting to fall in love, the insecurity of my teenage years and the sense of homelessness, the way I lost myself a bit with Paul and how that relationship ending led me to connect more with myself. It feels like all of those experiences have led me to this moment, this moment of complete joy, in which I've finally found my soulmate, the love of my life. I couldn't feel any luckier, or any more grateful that fate led me to Seb.

'You have made each other the promise of a life-long love and commitment. Seb and Rachel, it now gives me great pleasure to pronounce you husband and wife.' The registrar smiles. 'You may kiss your bride.'

Seb and I grin at each other and lean in for a kiss. I don't think I can ever remember being so happy. My wedding might be small, very small, but it's perfect.

The registrar congratulates us and we sign the register and pose for some photos. What was once a holiday romance is now official, in black and white. We thank the registrar and head outside, where we pose for some photos. The grey sky has cleared while we've been inside and the sun's come out. It's glowing down on us, twinkling in the sky, like it's giving us its blessing. Seb and I both gaze up at it before looking at each other and exchanging yet another happy smile.

We head up the road, chatting and laughing with our guests on our way to the pub. Our wedding might have been a small affair, but we're having a big celebration at one of the nicest London pubs. All of my friends are there, my best friends, Sasha and Julia from work, friends from university and my colleagues. Seb doesn't know as many people in London as I do yet, but a few friends he met while travelling who live in the UK have come to London and a couple of his best friends and relatives from back home have flown over. Everyone's waiting for us as we arrive. A big group of them are gathered in front of the pub, with smiles on their faces and bottles of champagne ready to uncork. A few of them are holding handfuls of confetti and throw them over us as we approach. Everyone's clapping and hollering and saying "congratulations". I can barely see through all the confetti as Seb and I smile for the pictures.

Eventually we make it into the pub, which we've booked out for the afternoon. There's an open bar and a buffet, with a towering wedding cake. We mingle with the guests, catching up with everyone. It's great to properly catch up with people who I've been away from for so long and it's nice to introduce Seb to the people he hasn't met yet. Like always, he gets along with everyone effortlessly.

'We need to call Cody, Joe and Helen!' I remind Seb after a few drinks.

'Oh yeah!'

I find my mum and ask her for the iPad she's been carrying for me. We turn it on and connect to the pub's WiFi. We log onto Zoom and call Helen first.

She picks up after a few rings. She's sitting outdoors, a backdrop of lush trees behind her. She's wearing the white ashram robes and looks tanned and content. She's been in the ashram for about a month now and we've been messaging back and forth on Facebook. I wouldn't say we're best friends, but I've grown to like her. Now that the Seb awkwardness is out of the way, we've been getting on pretty well. She's been keeping me up-to-date on life in the ashram and it's been nice to share her journey with her and give her tips on life over there. She seems to be really loving the experience, getting heavily into meditation. She hasn't met a guy yet, but I think she's beginning to realise that relationships aren't everything, like I did when I stayed there. Like me, she's coming to the conclusion that the most important relationship of all is the one you have with yourself.

She takes me and Seb in, her eyes lighting up. She claps her hand over her mouth. She looks genuinely thrilled for us.

'You guys look gorgeous! Congratulations!' she says.

'Thanks Helen!' I enthuse.

'I'm so happy for you!' She smiles.

'Thanks, we appreciate it!' Seb says. 'You're looking well. How's life over in India?'

'It's great, but tell me about your big day! Show me the pub!' Helen says, pronouncing the word "pub" in a funny English accent.

We pan the iPad around the room so she can see the guests and take in the atmosphere.

'Oh wow, it looks so much fun! I haven't had a drink in weeks!' she comments wistfully.

I laugh. 'Yeah, getting alcohol in the ashram is like trying to find water in a desert.'

'Exactly!'

'Let's get Cody and Joe on the call!' I suggest.

'Oh, do!' Helen enthuses.

We connect to Cody and Joe, who are now in Tibet. They've been trekking and visiting temples and from the look of the pictures they post on Facebook when they have the chance, they've been having an incredible time. When they answer, they're sitting in a hotel room, a dark sky visible through the window behind them since Tibet is eight hours ahead of the UK. They're sitting close, Joe lying in Cody's arms. They still seem really into each other, even if they haven't gone public on Facebook yet, but hopefully they will in time.

Joe lets out a squeal when he sees us. 'Guys! Congratulations!'

We grin back, telling them about our little ceremony and showing them the pub, like we did with Helen. They're happy to see Helen too and we all spend a few minutes catching up.

'We have some news,' Seb says eventually.

'What's that?' Cody asks.

'One sec!' Seb hands the iPad to my mum who holds it so that Cody, Joe and Helen can see what's going on.

I tap my spoon against my champagne glass a few times until the room falls silent.

I look at Seb, feeling that fluttery nervous and excited feeling again. He gives me an encouraging smile.

I clear my throat.

'We wanted to make a speech,' I say, as everyone turns to look at us.

'We want to say thank you to all of you for being here for us today. It might not be a typical wedding, but we're having the best time and we hope you are too. It means a lot to us to have so many friends and family come to celebrate with us, including Seb's dad Greg and his best friend Alex, who have come all the way from Montreal. And the lovely Meera, who saw that Seb and I were meant to be together before we even realised it ourselves and acted as Cupid back in the ashram. Thanks so much to Meera and her lovely husband John for coming all the way from India to be with us today.'

I exchange a soppy smile with Meera. A few inebriated guests let out a 'whoop'.

'I always thought my life would follow a conventional path. I thought I'd have a church wedding and be married by thirty,' I say, going off on a tangent I hadn't discussed with Seb when we planned this speech. 'Never in a million years did I think I'd end up finding the love of my life in an ashram in India!' I exclaim. 'And never did I think I'd get married in an orange dress!'

Our guests laugh.

'And yet every single thing about today is perfect. Wilder than my wildest dreams, literally. I couldn't be marrying a better man and I'm so glad I rocked up in India completely clueless, because in going far, far away, I finally found my home.'

I put my hand on Seb's chest and smile up at him.

A few guests make 'aww' noises and a few flashes go off as several of them take our picture.

Priya is crying again and I glance at the iPad to see that even Helen and Joe have also teared up. Cody smiles, looking touched too.

'I never thought I'd meet the love of my life at an ashram, either!' Seb says. 'In fact, I went to the ashram to have a year of total abstinence. Abstaining from alcohol, sex, all my vices, and then Rachel came along, and well, ruined it! In the best way possible!' Seb grins.

Our guests laugh even more.

Seb continues. 'I've had relationships before and I thought I'd been in love, but with Rachel it was completely different. I was looking for something in India. I was looking for some kind of enlightenment. I thought I'd touch another spiritual plane through meditation during my time over there, but I found pure happiness in Rachel instead. What can be more enlightening than love?'

My heart swells. I flick a tear from my eye and lean in to kiss him.

'To Seb and Rachel!' My dad says and everyone echoes, raising their glasses in a toast.

The murmur of chatter picks up again, but Seb and I aren't done.

I tap my spoon on my glass again.

'We have something else we want to tell you, actually' I say, feeling a nervous flutter.

Everyone looks at us curiously.

'I'm... I'm pregnant,' I say.

Delight spreads over our guests' faces.

Seb smiles proudly. 'We're going to start a family!' he adds.

A chorus of congratulations follows our announcement. Priya gawps at me. This is the first time I've told anyone apart from my parents, who have kept it secret. Greg knew too but it's news to everyone else, even Meera, who shrieks with joy.

When we first got back to England, I started feeling sick, almost like I'd felt when Seb and I arrived in Nepal from India. We thought maybe it was a diet thing and that I'd eaten something weird in Nepal that had given me food poisoning again. I was sick for a few days, but then it dawned on us both that I was only getting ill in the mornings. I'd been on the pill over in India and Nepal, but I found out from a google search that its effects are weakened by getting food poisoning. My doctor confirmed the same. Neither Seb or I had been thinking about having a baby. I thought it might be on the cards further down the line, but it had barely occurred to me as a priority, and yet the moment we found out, we were both overjoyed. It felt like a gleaming cherry on top of our beautiful cake. Seb can't wait. He's been coming to all the antenatal appointments with me and he's even started stockpiling baby clothes and turning the spare room into the baby's room. He found a cot on eBay and he's been filling the baby's room with teddy bears and toys. He's so excited to be a dad and I can't wait to be a mum either. I've always been more focused on my career than motherhood and yet ever since we found out that I'm pregnant, I've felt completely confident that being a mum is exactly what I want. I think it just never felt quite right before, because I hadn't found the right person to be a mum with. But now I have Seb and I can't wait to start a family.

'To Rachel, Seb and their baby!' My dad says, smiling from ear to ear.

Our guests echo his toast.

I look up at Seb, my husband and the father of my baby, and I realise that what I once thought was a holiday romance, really has gone the distance.

    'I love you,' Seb says.

    'I love you too,' I reply as I lean in for a kiss.

Printed in Great Britain
by Amazon